🔥 **Chronicles** *of* **Ancient Darkness** 🔥

WOLF
BROTHER

Chronicles of Ancient Darkness

WOLF BROTHER

BOOK ONE

MICHELLE PAVER

HARPERCOLLINS*PUBLISHERS*

www.harperchildrens.com

Library of Congress Cataloging-in-Publication Data
Paver, Michelle.
　Chronicles of ancient darkness: Wolf brother / by Michelle Paver.—1st
American ed.
　　p.　　cm.—(Chronicles of ancient darkness ; bk. 1)
　Summary: 6,000 years ago, twelve-year-old Torak and his guide, a wolf cub,
set out on a dangerous journey to fulfill an oath the boy made to his dying
father—to travel to the Mountain of the World Spirit to destroy a demon-
possessed bear that threatens all the clans.
　ISBN 0-06-072825-6 — ISBN 0-06-072826-4 (lib. bdg.)
　[1. Voyages and travels—Fiction. 2. Prehistoric people—Fiction.
3. Wolves—Fiction. 4. Demoniac possession—Fiction. 5. Bears—Fiction.]
I. Title. II. Series.
PZ7.P2853Wo 2005　　　　　　　　　　　　　　　　　2004008857
[Fic]—dc22　　　　　　　　　　　　　　　　　　　　　　CIP
　　　　　　　　　　　　　　　　　　　　　　　　　　　AC

Book design by Amy Ryan
1 2 3 4 5 6 7 8 9 10
❖
First American Edition
First published in Great Britain in 2004 by Orion Children's Books,
a division of the Orion Publishing Group Ltd.

Chronicles *of* Ancient Darkness

WOLF
BROTHER

ONE

Torak woke with a jolt from a sleep he'd never meant to have.

The fire had burned low. He crouched in the fragile shell of light and peered into the looming blackness of the Forest. He couldn't see anything. Couldn't hear anything. Had it come back? Was it out there now, watching him with its hot, murderous eyes?

He felt hollow and cold. He knew that he badly needed food, and that his arm hurt, and his eyes were scratchy with tiredness, but he couldn't really *feel* it. All night he'd guarded the wreck of the spruce bough shelter and watched his father bleed. How could this be happening?

Only yesterday—*yesterday*—they'd pitched camp in the blue autumn dusk. Torak had made a joke, and his father was laughing. Then the Forest exploded. Ravens screamed. Pines cracked. And out of the dark beneath the trees surged a deeper darkness: a huge rampaging menace in bear form.

Suddenly death was upon them. A frenzy of claws. A welter of sound to make the ears bleed. In a heartbeat, the creature had smashed their shelter to splinters. In a heartbeat, it had ripped a ragged wound in his father's side. Then it was gone, melting into the Forest as silently as mist.

But what kind of bear *stalks* men—then vanishes without making the kill? What kind of bear plays with its prey?

And where was it now?

Torak couldn't see beyond the firelight, but he knew that the clearing, too, was a wreck of snapped saplings and trampled bracken. He smelled pine-blood and clawed earth. He heard the soft, sad bubbling of the stream thirty paces away. The bear could be anywhere.

Beside him, his father moaned. Slowly he opened his eyes and looked at his son without recognition.

Torak's heart clenched. "Fa, it—it's me," he stammered. "How do you feel?"

Pain convulsed his father's lean brown face. His

cheeks were tinged with gray, making the clan-tattoos stand out lividly. Sweat matted his long dark hair.

His wound was so deep that as Torak clumsily stanched it with beard-moss, he saw his father's guts glistening in the firelight. He had to grit his teeth to keep from retching. He hoped Fa didn't notice—but of course he did. Fa was a hunter. He noticed everything.

"Torak . . ." he breathed. His hand reached out, his hot fingers clinging to Torak's as eagerly as a child. Torak swallowed. Sons clutch their fathers' hands, not the other way around.

He tried to be practical: to be a man instead of a boy. "I've still got some yarrow leaves," he said, fumbling for his medicine pouch with his free hand. "Maybe that'll stop the—"

"Keep it. You're bleeding too."

"Doesn't hurt," lied Torak. The bear had thrown him against a birch tree, bruising his ribs and gashing his left forearm.

"Torak—leave. Now. Before it comes back."

Torak stared at him. He opened his mouth but no sound came.

"You must," said his father.

"No. *No.* I can't—"

"Torak—I'm dying. I'll be dead by sunrise."

Torak gripped the medicine pouch. There was a roaring in his ears. "Fa—"

"Give me—what I need for the Death Journey. Then get your things."

The Death Journey. No. No.

But his father's face was stern. "My bow," he said. "Three arrows. You—keep the rest. Where I'm going—hunting's easy."

There was a tear in the knee of Torak's buckskin leggings. He dug his thumbnail into the flesh. It hurt. He forced himself to concentrate on that.

"Food," gasped his father. "The dried meat. You—take it all."

Torak's knee had started to bleed. He kept digging. He tried not to picture his father on the Death Journey. He tried not to picture himself alone in the Forest. He was only twelve summers old. He couldn't survive on his own. He didn't know how.

"Torak! Move!"

Blinking furiously, Torak reached for his father's weapons and laid them by his side. He divided up the arrows, pricking his fingers on the sharp flint points. Then he shouldered his quiver and bow and scrabbled in the wreckage for his small black basalt axe. His hazelwood pack had been smashed in the attack; he'd have to cram everything else into his jerkin, or tie it to his belt.

He reached for his reindeer-hide sleeping-sack.

"Take mine," murmured his father. "You never

did—repair yours. And—swap knives."

Torak was aghast. "Not your knife! You'll need it!"

"You'll need it more. And—it'll be good to have something of yours on the Death Journey."

"Fa, please. Don't—"

In the Forest, a twig snapped.

Torak spun round.

The darkness was absolute. Everywhere he looked the shadows were bear-shaped.

No wind.

No birdsong.

Just the crackle of the fire and the thud of his heart. The Forest itself was holding its breath.

His father licked the sweat from his lips. "It's not here yet," he said. "Soon. It will come for me soon. . . . Quick. The knives."

Torak didn't want to swap knives. That would make it final. But his father was watching him with an intensity that allowed no refusal.

Clenching his jaw so hard that it hurt, Torak took his own knife and put it into Fa's hand. Then he untied the buckskin sheath from his father's belt. Fa's knife was beautiful and deadly, with a blade of banded blue slate shaped like a willow leaf, and a haft of red deer antler that was bound with elk sinew for a better grip. As Torak looked down at it, the truth hit him. He was getting ready for a life without Fa. "I'm not leaving you!" he cried. "I'll fight it, I—"

"No! No one can fight this bear!"

Ravens flew up from the trees.

Torak forgot to breathe.

"Listen to me," hissed his father. "A bear—any bear—is the strongest hunter in the Forest. You know that. But this bear—*much* stronger."

Torak felt the hairs on his arms rise. Looking down into his father's eyes, he saw the tiny scarlet veins and, at the centers, the fathomless dark. "What do you mean?" he whispered. "What—"

"It is—possessed." His father's face was grim; he didn't seem like Fa anymore. "Some—demon—from the Otherworld—has entered it and made it evil."

An ember spat. The dark trees leaned closer to listen.

"A *demon*?" said Torak.

His father shut his eyes, mustering his strength. "It lives only to kill," he said at last. "With each kill—its power will grow. It will slaughter—everything. The prey. The clans. All will die. The Forest will die—" He broke off. "In one moon—it will be too late. The demon—too strong."

"One moon? But what—"

"Think, Torak! When the red eye is highest in the night sky, that's when demons are strongest. You know this. That's when the bear will be—invincible." He fought for breath. In the firelight, Torak saw the pulse beating in his throat. So faint: as if it might stop at any moment. "I need you—to swear something," said Fa.

"Anything."

Fa swallowed. "Head north. Many daywalks. Find—the Mountain—of the World Spirit."

Torak stared at him. *What?*

His father's eyes opened, and he gazed into the branches overhead, as if he saw things there that no one else could. "Find it," he said again. "It's the only hope."

"But—no one's ever found it. No one can."

"You can."

"How? I don't—"

"Your guide—will find you."

Torak was bewildered. Never before had his father talked like this. He was a practical man; a hunter. "I don't understand any of this!" he cried. "What guide? Why must I find the Mountain? Will I be safe there? Is that it? Safe from the bear?"

Slowly, Fa's gaze left the sky and came to rest on his son's face. He looked as if he was wondering how much more Torak could take. "Ah, you're too young," he said. "I thought I had more time. So much I haven't told you. Don't—don't hate me for that later."

Torak looked at him in horror. Then he leaped to his feet. "I can't do this on my own. Shouldn't I try to find—"

"No!" said his father with startling force. "All your

life I've kept you apart. Even—from our own Wolf Clan. Stay away from men! If they find out—what you can do . . ."

"What do you mean? I don't—"

"No time," his father cut in. "Now swear. On my knife. Swear that you will find the Mountain, or die trying."

Torak bit his lip hard. East through the trees, a gray light was growing. Not yet, he thought in panic. *Please* not yet.

"Swear," hissed his father.

Torak knelt and picked up the knife. It was heavy: a man's knife, too big for him. Awkwardly he touched it to the wound on his forearm. Then he put it to his shoulder, where the strip of wolf fur, his clan-creature, was sewn to his jerkin. In an unsteady voice he took his oath. "I swear, by my blood on this blade, and by each of my three souls—that I will find the Mountain of the World Spirit. Or die trying."

His father breathed out. "Good. Good. Now. Put the Death Marks on me. Hurry. The bear—not far off."

Torak felt the salty sting of tears. Angrily he brushed them away. "I haven't got any ochre," he mumbled.

"Take—mine."

In a blur, Torak found the little antler-tine medicine horn that had been his mother's. In a blur, he yanked out the black oak stopper, and shook some of the red ochre into his palm.

Suddenly he stopped. "I can't."

"You can. For me."

Torak spat into his palm and made a sticky paste of the ochre, the dark-red blood of the earth; then he drew the small circles on his father's skin that would help the souls recognize each other and stay together after death.

First, as gently as he could, he removed his father's beaver-hide boots and drew a circle on each heel, to mark the name-soul. Then he drew another circle over the heart, to mark the clan-soul. This wasn't easy, as his father's chest was scarred from an old wound, so Torak managed only a lopsided oval. He hoped that would be good enough.

Last, he made the most important mark of all: a circle on the forehead to mark the Nanuak, the world-soul. By the time he'd finished, he was swallowing tears.

"Better," murmured his father. But Torak saw with a clutch of terror that the pulse in his throat was fainter.

"You can't die!" Torak burst out.

His father gazed at him with pain and longing.

"Fa, I'm not leaving you, I—"

"Torak. You swore an oath." Again he closed his eyes. "Now. You—keep the medicine horn. I don't need it anymore. Take your things. Fetch me water from the river. Then—go."

I will *not* cry, Torak told himself as he rolled up his

father's sleeping-sack and tied it across his back; jammed his axe into his belt; stuffed his medicine pouch into his jerkin.

He got to his feet and looked about for the waterskin. It was ripped to shreds. He'd have to bring water in a dock leaf. He was about to go when his father murmured his name.

Torak turned. "Yes, Fa?"

"Remember. When you're hunting, look behind you. I—always tell you." He forced a smile. "You always—forget. Look behind you. Yes?"

Torak nodded. He tried to smile back. Then he blundered through the wet bracken toward the stream.

The light was growing, and the air smelled fresh and sweet. Around him the trees were bleeding: oozing golden pine-blood from the slashes the bear had inflicted. Some of the tree-spirits were moaning quietly in the dawn breeze.

Torak reached the stream, where mist floated above the bracken, and willows trailed their fingers in the cold water. Glancing quickly around, he snatched a dock leaf and moved forward, his boots sinking into the soft red mud.

He froze.

Beside his right boot was the track of a bear. A front paw: twice the size of his own head, and so fresh that he could see the points where the long, vicious claws had bitten deep into the mud.

Look behind you, Torak.

He spun round.

Willows. Alder. Fir.

No bear.

A raven flew down onto a nearby bough, making him jump. The bird folded its stiff black wings and fixed him with a beady eye. Then it jerked its head, croaked once, and flew away.

Torak stared in the direction it had seemed to indicate.

Dark yew. Dripping spruce. Dense. Impenetrable.

But deep within—no more than ten paces away—a stir of branches. Something was in there. Something huge.

He tried to keep his panicky thoughts from skittering away, but his mind had gone white.

The thing about a bear, his father always said, *is that it can move as silently as breath. It could be watching you from ten paces away, and you'd never know. Against a bear you have no defenses. You can't run faster. You can't climb higher. You can't fight it on your own. All you can do is learn its ways, and try to persuade it that you're neither threat nor prey.*

Torak forced himself to stay still. Don't run. Don't run. Maybe it doesn't know you're here.

A low hiss. Again the branches stirred.

He heard the stealthy rustle as the creature moved toward the shelter: toward his father. He waited in rigid silence as it passed. Coward! he shouted inside his head. You let it go without even trying to save Fa!

But what could you do? said the small part of his mind that could still think straight. Fa knew this would happen. That's why he sent you for water. He knew it was coming for him. . . .

"Torak!" came his father's wild cry. *"Run!"*

Crows burst from the trees. A roar shook the Forest—on and on till Torak's head was splitting.

"Fa!" he screamed.

"Run!"

Again the Forest shook. Again came his father's cry. Then suddenly it broke off.

Torak jammed his fist in his mouth.

Through the trees, he glimpsed a great dark shadow in the wreck of the shelter.

He turned and ran.

TWO

Torak crashed through alder thickets and sank to his knees in bogs. Birch trees whispered of his passing. Silently he begged them not to tell the bear.

The wound in his arm burned, and with each breath his bruised ribs ached savagely, but he didn't dare stop. The Forest was full of eyes. He pictured the bear coming after him. He ran on.

He startled a young boar grubbing up pignuts, and grunted a quick apology to ward off an attack. The boar gave an ill-tempered snort and let him pass.

A wolverine snarled at him to stay *away*, and he snarled back as fiercely as he could, because wolverines only listen to threats. The wolverine decided he meant it and shot up a tree.

To the east, the sky was wolf gray. Thunder growled. In the stormy light, the trees were a brilliant green. Rain in the mountains, thought Torak numbly. Watch out for flash floods.

He forced himself to think of that—to push away the horror. It didn't work. He ran on.

At last, he had to stop for breath. He collapsed against an oak tree. As he raised his head to stare at the shifting green leaves, the tree murmured secrets to itself, shutting him out.

For the first time in his life, he was truly alone. He didn't feel part of the Forest anymore. He felt as if his world-soul had snapped its link to all other living things: tree and bird, hunter and prey, river and rock. Nothing in the whole world knew how he felt. Nothing wanted to know.

The pain in his arm wrenched him back from his thoughts. From his medicine pouch he took his last scrap of birch bast and roughly bandaged the wound. Then he pushed himself off the tree trunk and looked around.

He'd grown up in this part of the Forest. Every slope, every glade was familiar. In the valley to the west was the Redwater: too shallow for canoes, but good for fishing in spring, when the salmon come up from the Sea. To the east, all the way to the edge of the Deep

Forest, lay the vast sunlit woods where the prey grow fat in autumn, and berries and nuts are plentiful. To the south were the moors where the reindeer eat moss in winter.

Fa said that the best thing about this part of the Forest was that so few people came here. Maybe the odd party of Willow Clan from the west by the Sea, or Viper Clan up from the south, but they never stayed long. They simply passed through, hunting freely as everyone did in the Forest, and unaware that Torak and Fa hunted here too.

Torak had never questioned that before. It was how he'd always lived: alone with Fa, away from the clans. Now, though, he longed for people. He wanted to shout; to yell for help.

But Fa had warned him to stay away from them.

Besides, shouting might draw the bear.

The bear.

Panic rose in his throat. He pushed it down. He took a deep breath and started to run again, more steadily this time, heading north.

As he ran, he picked up signs of prey. Elk tracks. Auroch droppings. The sound of a forest horse moving through the bracken. The bear hadn't frightened them away. At least, not yet.

So had his father been wrong? Had his wits been wandering at the end?

"Your fa's mad!" the children had taunted Torak five summers before, when he and Fa had journeyed to the seashore for the yearly clan meet. It was Torak's first-ever clan meet, and it had been a disaster. Fa had never taken him again.

"They say he swallowed the breath of a ghost," the children had sneered. "That's why he left his clan and lives on his own."

Torak had been furious. He would've fought them all if his father hadn't come along and hauled him off. "Torak, ignore them." Fa had laughed. "They don't know what they're saying."

He'd been right, of course.

But was he right about the bear?

Up ahead, the trees opened into a clearing. Torak stumbled into the sun—and into a stench of rottenness.

He lurched to a halt.

The forest horses lay where the bear had tossed them like broken playthings. No scavenger had dared feed on them. Not even the flies would touch them.

They looked like no bear kill Torak had ever seen. When a normal bear feeds, it peels back the hide of its prey and takes the innards and hind parts, then caches the rest for later. Like any other hunter, it wastes nothing. But this bear had ripped no more than a single bite from each carcass. It hadn't killed from hunger. It had killed for fun.

At Torak's feet lay a dead foal, its small hooves still crusted with river clay from its final drink. His gorge rose. What kind of creature slaughters an entire herd? What kind of creature kills for pleasure?

He remembered the bear's eyes, glimpsed for one appalling heartbeat. He'd never seen such eyes. Behind them lay nothing but endless rage and a hatred of all living things. The hot, churning chaos of the Otherworld.

Of course his father was right. This wasn't a bear. It was a demon. It would kill and kill until the Forest was dead.

No one can fight this bear, his father had said. Did that mean the Forest was doomed? And why did he, Torak, have to find the Mountain of the World Spirit? The Mountain that no one had ever seen?

His father's voice echoed in his mind. *Your guide will find you.*

How? When?

Torak left the glade and plunged back into the shadows beneath the trees. Once again he began to run.

He ran forever. He ran till he could no longer feel his legs. But at last he reached a long, wooded slope and had to stop: doubled up, chest heaving.

Suddenly he was ravenous. He fumbled for his food pouch—and groaned in disgust. It was empty. Too late, he remembered the neat bundles of dried deer meat, forgotten at the shelter.

Torak, you fool! Messing things up on your first day alone! Alone.

It wasn't possible. How could Fa be gone? Gone forever?

Gradually he became aware of a faint mewing sound coming from the other side of the hill.

There it was again. Some young animal crying for its mother.

His heart leaped. Oh, thank the Spirit! An easy kill. His belly tightened at the thought of fresh meat. He didn't care what it was. He was so hungry he could eat a bat.

Torak dropped to the ground and crept through the birch trees to the top of the hill.

He looked down into a narrow gully through which ran a small, swift river. He recognized it: the Fastwater. Farther west, he and Fa often camped in summer to gather lime bark for rope making; but this part looked unfamiliar. Then he realized why.

Some time before, a flash flood had come roaring down from the mountains. The waters had since subsided, leaving a mess of wet undergrowth and grass-strewn saplings. They'd also destroyed a wolf den on the other side of the gully. There, below a big red boulder shaped like a sleeping auroch, lay two drowned wolves like sodden fur cloaks. Three dead cubs floated in a puddle.

The fourth sat beside them, shivering.

The wolf cub looked about three moons old. It was thin and wet, and was complaining softly to itself in a low, continuous whimper.

Torak flinched. Without warning, the sound had brought a startling vision to his mind. Black fur. Warm darkness. Rich, fatty milk. The Mother licking him clean. The scratch of tiny claws and nudge of small, cold noses. Fluffy cubs clambering over him: the newest cub in the litter.

The vision was as vivid as a lightning flash. What did it mean?

His hand tightened on his father's knife. It doesn't matter what it means, he told himself. Visions won't keep you alive. If you don't eat that cub, you'll be too weak to hunt. And you're allowed to kill your clan-creature to keep from starving. You know that.

The cub raised its head and gave a bewildered yowl.

Torak listened to it—*and understood.*

In some strange way that he couldn't begin to fathom, he recognized the high, wavering sounds. His mind knew their shapes. He remembered them.

This isn't possible, he thought.

He listened to the cub's yowls. He felt them drop into his mind.

Why won't you play with me? the cub was asking its dead pack. *What have I done now?*

On and on it went. As Torak listened, something awakened in him. His neck muscles tensed. Deep in his throat he felt a response beginning. He fought the urge to put back his head and howl.

What was happening? He didn't feel like Torak anymore. Not boy, not son, not member of the Wolf Clan— or not *only* those things. Some part of him was wolf.

A breeze sprang up, chilling his skin.

At the same moment, the wolf cub stopped yowling and jerked round to face him. Its eyes were unfocused, but its large ears were pricked, and it was snuffing the air. It had smelled him.

Torak looked down at the small anxious cub and hardened his heart.

He drew the knife from his belt and started down the slope.

THREE

The wolf cub did not *at all* understand what was going on.

He'd been exploring the rise above the Den when the Fast Wet had come roaring through, and now his mother and father and pack-brothers were lying in the mud—*and they were ignoring him.*

Since long before the Light he'd been nosing them and biting their tails—but they still didn't move. They didn't make a sound, and they smelled strange: like prey. Not the prey that runs away, but the Not-Breath kind: the kind that gets eaten.

The cub was cold, wet, and very hungry. Many

times he'd licked his mother's muzzle to ask her please to sick up some food for him to eat, but she didn't stir. What had he done wrong this time?

He knew that he was the naughtiest cub in the litter. He was always being scolded, but he couldn't help it. He just loved trying new things. So it seemed a bit unfair that now, when he was staying by the Den like a good cub, nobody even noticed.

He padded to the edge of the puddle where his pack-brothers lay and lapped up some of the Still Wet. It tasted bad.

He ate some grass and a couple of spiders.

He wondered what to do next.

He began to feel scared. He put back his head and howled. Howling cheered him up a bit, because it reminded him of all the good howls he'd had with the pack.

Mid-howl he stopped. He smelled wolf.

He spun around, wobbling a little from hunger. He swiveled his ears and sniffed. Yes. *Wolf.* He could hear it coming noisily down the slope on the other side of the Fast Wet. He smelled that it was male, half grown, and not one of the pack.

But there was something odd about it. It smelled of wolf, but also of not-wolf. It smelled of reindeer and red deer and beaver, and fresh blood—and something else: a new smell that he hadn't yet learned.

This was very odd. Unless—*unless*—it meant that
the not-wolf wolf was actually a wolf who'd eaten lots
of different prey, and was now bringing the cub some
food!

Shivering with eagerness, the cub wagged his tail
and yipped a noisy welcome.

For a moment the strange wolf stopped. Then it
moved forward again. The cub couldn't see it very
clearly because his eyes weren't nearly as sharp as his
nose and ears, but as it splashed across the Fast Wet, he
made out that this was a *very* strange wolf indeed.

It walked on its hind legs. The fur on its head was
black, and so long that it reached right down to its
shoulders. And strangest of all—*it had no tail!*

Yet it *sounded* wolf. It was making a low, friendly yip-
and-yowl which sounded a bit like *It's all right, I'm a
friend*. This was reassuring, even if it did keep missing
out the highest yips.

But something was wrong. Beneath the friendliness
there was a tense note. And although the strange wolf
was smiling, the cub could tell it didn't really mean it.

The cub's welcome changed to a whimper. *Are you
hunting me? Why?*

No, no came the friendly but not-friendly yip-and-
yowl.

Then the strange wolf stopped yip-and-yowling and
advanced in frightening silence.

Too weak to run, the cub backed away.

The strange wolf lunged, grabbed the cub by the scruff, and lifted him high.

Weakly, the cub wagged his tail to fend off an attack.

The strange wolf lifted its other forepaw and pressed a huge claw against the cub's belly.

The cub yelped. Grinning in terror, he whipped his tail between his legs.

But the strange wolf was frightened too. Its forepaws were shaking, and it was gulping and baring its teeth. The cub sensed loneliness and uncertainty and pain.

Suddenly, the strange wolf took another gulp, and jerked its great claw away from the cub's belly. Then it sat down heavily in the mud and clutched the cub to its chest.

The cub's terror vanished. Through the strange furless hide that smelled more of not-wolf than wolf, he could hear a comforting thump-thump, like the sound he heard when he clambered on top of his father for a nap.

The cub wriggled out of the strange wolf's grip, put his forepaws on its chest, and stood on his hind legs. He began to lick the strange wolf's muzzle.

Angrily, the strange wolf pushed him away, and he fell backward. Undeterred, he righted himself and sat gazing up at the strange wolf.

Such an odd, flat, furless face! The lips weren't black, like a proper wolf's, but pale; and the ears were pale too—*and they didn't move at all.* But the eyes were silver-gray and full of light: the eyes of a wolf.

The cub felt better than he had since the Fast Wet had come. He'd found a new pack-brother.

Torak was furious with himself. Why hadn't he killed the cub? Now what was he going to eat?

The cub jabbed its nose into his bruised ribs, making him yelp. "Get off!" he shouted, kicking it away. "I don't want you! You're no use! Go away!"

He didn't even attempt that in wolf talk, because he'd realized that he didn't actually speak it very well. He only knew the simpler gestures and some of the sound-shapes. But the cub picked up his meaning well enough. It trotted off a few paces, then sat down and looked at him hopefully, sweeping the ground with its tail.

Torak got to his feet—and the world tilted sickeningly. He had to eat soon.

He cast around the riverbank for food but saw only the dead wolves, and they smelled too bad even to think about. Hopelessness washed over him. The sun was getting low. What should he do? Camp here? But what about the bear? Had it finished with Fa and come after him?

Something twisted painfully in his chest. Don't think about Fa. Think what to do. If the bear had followed you, it would've got you by now. So maybe you'll be safe here—at least for tonight.

The wolf carcasses were too heavy to drag away, so he decided to camp farther upstream. First, though, he would use one of the carcasses to bait a deadfall, in the hope of trapping some food overnight.

It was a struggle to set the trap: to prop up a flat rock on a stick, then slot in another stick crossways to act as a trigger. If he was lucky, a fox might come along in the night and bring down the rock. It wouldn't make good eating, but it'd be better than nothing.

He'd just finished when the cub trotted over and gave the deadfall an inquisitive sniff. Torak grabbed its muzzle and slammed it to the ground. "No!" he said firmly. "You stay away!"

The cub shook itself and retired with an offended air.

Better offended than dead, thought Torak.

He knew he'd been unfair: He should've growled first to warn the cub to stay away, and only muzzle-grabbed if it hadn't listened. But he was too tired to worry about that.

Besides, why had he bothered to warn it at all? What did he care if it wobbled along in the night and got squashed? What did he care if he could understand it, or why? What use was that?

He stood up, and his knees nearly gave way. Forget about the cub. Find something to eat.

He forced himself to climb the slope behind the big red rock to look for cloudberries. Only when he got there did he remember that cloudberries grow on moors and marshes, not in birch woods, and that it was too late in the year for them anyway.

He noticed that in certain spots the ground was littered with wood grouse droppings, so he set some snares of twisted grass: two near the ground, and two on the sort of low branch that wood grouse sometimes run along—taking care to hide the snares with leaves so that the wood grouse wouldn't spot them. Then he went back to the river.

He knew he was too unsteady to try spearing a fish, so instead he set up a line of bramble-thorn fishing hooks baited with water snails. Then he started upriver to look for berries and roots.

For a while the cub followed him; then it sat down and mewed at him to come back. It didn't want to leave its pack.

Good, thought Torak. You stay there. I don't want you pestering me.

As he searched, the sun sank lower. The air grew sharp. His jerkin glistened with the misty breath of the Forest. He had a hazy thought that he should be building a shelter instead of looking for food, but he pushed it away.

At last he found a handful of crowberries and gulped them down. Then some late lingonberries; a couple of snails; a clutch of yellow bog mushrooms—a bit maggoty, but not too bad.

It was nearly dusk when he got lucky and found a clump of pignuts. With a sharp stick he dug down carefully, following the winding stems to the small, knobbly root. He chewed the first one: It tasted sweet and nutty but was barely a mouthful. After much exhausting digging, he grubbed up four more, ate two, and stuffed two in his jerkin for later.

With food inside him, a little strength returned to his limbs, but his mind was still strangely unclear. What do I do next? he wondered. Why is it so hard to think?

Shelter. That's it. Then fire. Then sleep.

The cub was waiting for him in the clearing. Shivering and yipping with delight, it threw itself at him with a big wolf-smile. It didn't just wrinkle its muzzle and draw back its lips; it smiled with its whole body. It slicked back its ears and tilted its head to one side; it waved its tail and waggled its forepaws, and made great twisting leaps in the air.

Watching it made Torak giddy, so he ignored it. Besides, he needed to build a shelter.

He looked around for deadwood, but the flood had

washed most of it away. He'd have to cut down some saplings, if he still had the strength.

Pulling his axe from his belt, he went over to a clump of birch and put his hand on the smallest. He muttered a quick warning to the tree's spirit to find another home fast, then started to chop.

The effort made his head swim. The cut on his forearm throbbed savagely. He forced himself to keep chopping.

He was in an endless dark tunnel of chopping and stripping branches and more chopping. But when his arms had turned to water and he could chop no more, he saw with alarm that he'd only managed to cut down two spindly birch saplings and a puny little spruce.

They'd have to do.

He lashed the saplings together with a split spruce root to make a low, rickety lean-to; then he covered it on three sides with spruce boughs and dragged in a few more to lie on.

It was pretty hopeless, but it'd have to do. He didn't have the strength to rainproof it with leaf mold. If it rained, he'd have to trust his sleeping-sack to keep him dry, and pray that the river-spirit didn't send another flood, because he'd built the shelter too close to the water.

Munching another pignut, he scanned the clearing for firewood. But he'd only just swallowed the pignut when his belly heaved, and he spewed it up again.

The cub yipped with delight and gulped down the sick.

Why did I do that? thought Torak. Did I eat a bad mushroom?

But it didn't feel like a bad mushroom. It felt like something else. He was sweating and shivering, and although there was nothing left in his belly to throw up, he still felt sick.

A horrible suspicion gripped him. He unwound the bandage on his forearm—and fear settled on him like an icy fog. The wound was a swollen, angry red. It smelled bad. He could feel the heat coming off it. When he touched it, pain flared.

A sob rose in his chest. He was exhausted, hungry, and frightened, and he desperately wanted Fa. And now he had a new enemy.

Fever.

FOUR

Torak had to make a fire. It was a race between him and the fever. The prize was his life.

He fumbled at his belt for his tinder pouch. His hands shook as he took out some wisps of shredded birch bark, and he kept dropping his flint and missing his strike-fire. He was snarling with frustration when he finally got a spark to take.

By the time he had a fire going, he was shivering uncontrollably and hardly felt the heat of the flames. Noises boomed unnaturally loud: the gurgle of the river, the *hoo-hoo* of an owl; the famished yipping of that infuriating cub. Why couldn't it leave him alone?

He staggered to the river for water. Just in time, he remembered what Fa said about not leaning over too far. *When you're ill, never catch sight of your name-soul in the water. Seeing it makes you dizzy. You might fall in and drown.*

With his eyes shut, he drank his fill, then stumbled back to the shelter. He longed for rest, but he knew that he had to see to his arm or he wouldn't stand a chance.

He took some dried willow bark from his medicine pouch and chewed it, gagging on its gritty bitterness. He smeared the paste on his forearm, then bound up the wound again with the birch-bast bandage. The pain was so bad that he nearly passed out. It was all he could do to kick off his boots and crawl into his sleeping-sack. The cub tried to clamber in too. He pushed it away.

Dully, teeth chattering, he watched the cub pad over to the fire and study it curiously. It extended one large gray paw and patted the flames—then leaped back with an outraged yelp.

"That'll teach you," muttered Torak.

The cub shook itself and bounded off into the gloom.

Torak curled into a ball, cradling his throbbing arm and thinking bitterly what a mess he'd made of things.

All his life he'd lived in the Forest with Fa, pitching camp for a night or two, then moving on. He knew the rules. *Never skimp on your shelter. Never use more effort than you need when gathering food. Never leave it too late to pitch camp.*

His first day on his own, and he'd broken every one. It was frightening. Like forgetting how to walk.

With his good hand, he touched his clan-tattoos, tracing the pair of fine dotted lines that followed each cheekbone. Fa had given them to him when he was seven, rubbing bearberry juice into the pierced skin. You don't deserve them, Torak told himself. If you die, it'll be your own fault.

Again the grief twisted in his chest. Never in his life had he slept alone. Never without Fa. For the first time, there was no good-night touch of the rough, gentle hand. No familiar smell of buckskin and sweat.

Torak's eyes began to sting. He screwed them shut and slid down into evil dreams.

He is wading knee-deep in moss, struggling to escape the bear. His father's screams ring in his ears. The bear is coming for him.

He tries to run, but he only sinks deeper into the moss. It sucks him down. His father is screaming.

The bear's eyes burn with the lethal fire of the Otherworld—the demon fire. It rears on its hind legs: a towering menace, unimaginably huge. Its great jaws gape as it roars its hatred to the moon. . . .

Torak woke with a cry.

The last of the bear's roars were echoing through the Forest. They weren't a dream. They were real.

Torak held his breath. He saw the blue moonlight through the gaps in his shelter. He saw that the fire was nearly out. He felt his heart pounding.

Again the Forest shook. The trees tensed to listen. But this time Torak realized that the roars were far away: many daywalks to the west. Slowly he breathed out.

At the mouth of the shelter, the cub sat watching him. Its slanted eyes were a strange, dark gold. Amber, thought Torak, remembering the little seal amulet that Fa had worn on a thong around his neck.

He found that oddly reassuring. At least he wasn't alone.

As his heartbeats returned to normal, the pain of his fever came surging back. It crisped his skin. His skull felt ready to burst. He struggled to get more willow bark from his medicine pouch, but dropped it and couldn't find it again in the half darkness. He dragged another branch onto the fire, then lay back, gasping.

He couldn't get those roars out of his head. Where was the bear now? The glade of dead horses had been north of the stream where it had attacked Fa, but now the bear seemed to be in the west. Would it keep heading west? Or had it caught Torak's scent and turned back? How long before it got here—and found him lying helpless and sick?

A calm, steady voice seemed to whisper in his mind, almost as if Fa were with him. *If the bear does come, the cub will warn you. Remember, Torak: A wolf's nose is so keen that he can smell the breath of a fish. His ears are so sharp that he can hear the clouds pass.*

Yes, thought Torak, the cub will warn me. That's something. I want to die with my eyes open, facing the bear like a man. Like Fa.

Somewhere very far off, a dog barked. Not a wolf, but a dog.

Torak frowned. Dogs meant people, and there were no people in this part of the Forest.

Were there?

He sank into darkness. Back into the clutches of the bear.

FIVE

It was nearly dark when Torak woke up. He'd slept all day.

He felt weak and ragingly thirsty, but his wound was cooler and much less sore. The fever was gone.

So was the cub.

Torak was surprised to find himself wondering if it was all right. Why should he care? The cub was nothing to him.

He stumbled to the river and drank, then woke the slumbering fire with more wood. The effort left him trembling. He rested, and ate the last pignut and some sorrel leaves he'd found by the riverbank. They were tough and very sour, but strengthening.

Still the cub didn't come.

He thought about trying to summon it with a howl. But if it came, it would only ask for food. Besides, howling might attract the bear. So instead, he pulled on his boots and went to check the traps.

The fishhooks were empty except for one, which held the bones of a small fish, neatly nibbled clean. He was luckier with the snares. One held a wood grouse, struggling feebly. *Meat*.

Muttering a quick thank you to the bird's spirit, Torak snapped its neck, slit its belly, and gulped the warm liver down raw. It tasted bitter and slimy, but he was too famished to care.

Feeling slightly steadier, he tied the bird to his belt and went to check the deadfall.

To his relief, it contained no dead cub. The cub was sitting by its mother, prodding her stinking carcass with one paw. At Torak's approach, it started toward him, then looked back at the she-wolf, yipping indignantly. It wanted Torak to sort things out.

Torak sighed. How could he explain about death when he didn't understand it himself?

"Come on," he said, not bothering to speak wolf.

The cub's large ears swiveled to catch the sound.

"There's nothing here," Torak said impatiently. "Let's go."

Back at the shelter, he plucked and spitted the wood grouse, and set it to roast over the fire. The cub lunged for it.

Torak grabbed the cub's muzzle and slammed it to the ground. *No!* he growled. *It's mine!*

The cub lay obediently still, thumping its tail. When Torak released its muzzle, it rolled onto its back, baring its pale fluffy belly, and gave him a silent grin of apology. Then it scampered off to a safe distance, head politely lowered.

Torak nodded, satisfied. The cub had to learn that *he* was the lead wolf, or there'd be endless trouble in the future.

What future? he thought with a scowl. His future didn't include the cub.

The smell of roast meat drove all other thoughts away. Fat sizzled on the fire. His mouth watered. Quickly, he twisted one leg off the wood grouse and tucked it into the fork of a birch tree as an offering for his clan guardian; then he settled down to eat.

It was the best thing he'd ever tasted. He sucked every shred of meat and fat off the bones, and crunched up every morsel of crisp, salty skin. He forced himself to ignore the great amber eyes that watched every bite.

When he'd finished, he wiped his mouth on the back of his hand. The cub followed every move.

Torak blew out a long breath. "Oh, all *right*," he

muttered. He tore the remaining foot off the carcass and tossed it over.

The cub crunched it up in moments. Then it looked at Torak hopefully.

"I haven't got any more," he told it.

The cub yipped impatiently and glanced at the carcass in his hands.

He'd picked the bones clean, but they'd still make needles, fishhooks and broth; although without a cooking skin, he couldn't make any broth.

Sensing that he might be storing up trouble for himself, he tossed half the carcass to the cub.

The cub demolished it in its powerful jaws, then curled up and went instantly to sleep: a gently heaving ball of hot gray fur.

Torak wanted to sleep too, but he knew that he couldn't. As night fell and the cold came on, he sat staring into the fire. Now that he'd shaken off the fever and eaten some meat, he could think clearly at last.

He thought of the glade of dead horses, and the bear's demon-haunted eyes. *It is possessed,* Fa had said. *Some demon from the Otherworld has entered it and made it evil.*

But what actually *is* a demon? Torak wondered. He didn't know. He only knew that demons hate all living things and sometimes escape from the Otherworld, rising out of the ground to cause sickness and havoc.

As he thought about this, he realized that although he knew quite a lot about hunters and prey—about lynxes and wolverines, aurochs and horses and deer— he knew very little about the other creatures of the Forest.

He did know that clan guardians watch over camp- sites, and that ghosts moan in leafless trees on stormy nights, forever seeking the clans they have lost. He knew that the Hidden People live inside rocks and rivers, just as the clans live in shelters, and that they seem beautiful until they turn their backs, which are hollow as rotten trees.

As for the World Spirit who sends the rain and snow and prey—about that Torak knew least of all. Until now he'd never even thought about it. It was too remote: an unimaginably powerful spirit who lived far away on its Mountain; a spirit whom no one had ever seen, but who was said to walk by summer as a man with the antlers of a deer, and by winter as a woman with bare red willow branches for hair.

Torak bowed his head to his knees. The weight of his oath to Fa pressed down on him like a rock.

Suddenly, the cub sprang up with a tense grunt.

Torak leaped to his feet.

The cub's eyes were fixed on the darkness: ears rigid, hackles raised. Then it hurtled out of the firelight and disappeared.

Torak stood very still with his hand on Fa's knife. He felt the trees watching him. He heard them whispering to each other.

Somewhere not far off, a robin began to sing its plaintive night song. The cub reappeared: hackles down, muzzle soft, and smiling slightly.

Torak relaxed his grip on the knife. Whatever was out there had either gone or wasn't a threat. If the bear had been close, that robin wouldn't be singing. He knew that much.

He sat down again.

You've got to find the Mountain of the World Spirit within the next moon, he told himself. That's what Fa said. *When the red eye is highest . . . that's when demons are strongest. You know this.*

Yes, I do know it, thought Torak. I know about the red eye. I've seen it.

Every autumn, the Great Bull Auroch—the most powerful demon in the Otherworld—escapes into the night sky. At first he has his head down, pawing the earth, so that only the starry gleam of his shoulder can be seen. But as winter comes on, he rises and grows stronger. That's when you see his glittering horns and his bloodshot red eye. The red star of winter.

And in the Moon of Red Willow he rides highest, and evil is strongest. That's when the demons walk. *That's when the bear will be invincible.*

Glancing up through the branches, Torak saw the cold glint of stars. On the eastern horizon, just above the distant blackness of the High Mountains, he found it: the starry shoulder of the Great Auroch.

It was now the end of the Moon of Roaring Stags. In the next moon, the Blackthorn Moon, the red eye would appear, and the power of the bear would grow stronger. By the Moon of Red Willow, it would be invincible.

Head north, Fa had said. *Many daywalks.*

Torak didn't want to go farther north. That would take him out of the small patch of the Forest that he knew, and into the unknown. And yet—Fa must have believed that he stood a chance, or he wouldn't have made him swear.

He reached for a stick and poked the embers.

He knew that the High Mountains were far in the east, beyond the Deep Forest, and that they curved from north to south, arching out of the Forest like the spine of an enormous whale. And he knew that the World Spirit was said to live in the northernmost mountain. But no one had ever gotten close to it, for the Spirit always beat them back with howling blizzards and treacherous rockfalls.

All day, Torak had been fleeing north, but he was still only level with the southernmost roots of the High Mountains. He had no idea how he was going to get so far on his own. He was still weak from the fever, and in no state to start a journey.

So don't, he thought. Don't make the same mistake twice: Don't panic and nearly kill yourself out of sheer stupidity. Stay here for another day or so. Get stronger. Then start.

Making a decision made him feel a little better.

He put more sticks on the fire, and saw to his surprise that the cub was watching him. Its eyes were steady and quite un-cublike: the eyes of a wolf.

Once again, Fa's voice echoed in his memory. *The eyes of a wolf aren't like those of any other creature—except those of a man. Wolves are our closest brothers, Torak, and it shows in their eyes. The only difference is the color. Theirs are golden, while ours are gray. But the wolf doesn't see that, because his world doesn't have colors. Only silvers and grays.*

Torak had asked how he knew that, but Fa had smiled and shaken his head, saying he'd explain when Torak was older. There were lots of things he'd been going to explain when Torak was older.

Torak scowled and rubbed his face.

The cub was still watching him.

Already it had something of the beauty of a full-grown wolf: the slender pale-gray muzzle; large silver ears with their edging of black; elegant, dark-rimmed eyes.

Those eyes. As clear as sunlight in springwater . . .

Suddenly, Torak had the strangest sense that the cub knew what he was thinking.

More than any other hunters in the Forest, Fa whispered in his mind, *wolves are like us. They hunt in packs. They enjoy talking and playing. They have a fierce love for their mates and cubs. And each wolf works hard for the good of the pack.*

Torak sat upright. Was that what Fa was trying to tell him?

Your guide will find you.

Could it be that the cub was his guide?

He decided to put it to the test. Clearing his throat, he got down on his hands and knees. He didn't know how to say "mountain" in wolf talk, so he guessed: gesturing with his head and asking—in the low, intense yip-and-yowl that forms part of wolf talk—if the cub knew the way.

The cub swiveled its ears and looked at him, then glanced politely away, because in wolf talk, to stare too hard is a threat. Then it stood up, stretched, and lazily swung its tail.

Nothing in its movements told Torak that it had understood his question. It was simply a cub again.

Or was it?

Could he really have imagined that look?

SIX

It was many Lights and Darks since Tall Tailless had come.

At first he'd slept all the time, but now he was being more of a normal wolf. When he felt sad, he went quiet. When he was angry, he snarled. He liked playing tag with a bit of hare skin, and when the cub pounced on him he rolled on the ground, making odd yip-and-yowls which the cub guessed was his way of laughing.

Sometimes Tall Tailless would join the cub in a howl, and they'd sing their feelings to the Forest. Tall Tailless's howl was rough and not very tuneful, but full of feeling.

The rest of his talk was the same: rough but

expressive. Of course, he didn't have a tail, and he couldn't move his ears or fluff up his fur or hit the high yips. But he usually made himself understood.

So in many ways, he was just like any other wolf.

Although not in everything. Poor Tall Tailless could hardly smell or hear at all, and during the Dark he liked to stare at the Bright Beast-That-Bites-Hot. Sometimes he took his hind paws *right off*, and one terrible time even his pelt. Strangest of all, he slept for *ages*. He didn't seem to know that a wolf should only ever sleep in snatches, and must get up often, stretching and turning, so that he's ready for anything.

The cub tried to teach Tall Tailless to wake up more often, by nudging him and biting his ears. Instead of being grateful, Tall Tailless just got very, very cross. In the end the cub let him sleep; and next Light, Tall Tailless got up after a stupidly long sleep in an extremely bad mood. Well what did he expect, if he wouldn't let his pack-brother wake him up?

Today, though, Tall Tailless had woken up before the Light, and in a very different mood. The cub sensed his nervousness.

Curiously, the cub watched Tall Tailless set off along the pack trail that went up-Wet. A hunt?

The cub bounded after him, then yipped at him to stop. This wasn't a hunt. And Tall Tailless was going the wrong way.

It wasn't just that he was following the Fast Wet, which the cub now hated and feared more than anything. This was the wrong way because—because it wasn't the right way. The right way was over the hill, then on for many Lights and Darks.

The cub didn't know how he knew this, but he felt it inside: a faint, deep Pull—like the pull of the Den when he'd strayed too far, only fainter, because it was coming from so far away.

Up ahead, Tall Tailless strode along unaware.

The cub gave a low, warning "Uff!"—like his mother used to when she wanted them back in the Den *now*.

Tall Tailless turned round. He asked something in his own talk. It sounded like "Whatisit?"

"Uff!" snapped the cub. He trotted to the foot of the hill and stared at the right trail. Then he glanced at Tall Tailless, then back to the trail. *Not that way. This way.*

Impatiently, Tall Tailless repeated his question. The cub waited for him to catch on.

Tall Tailless scratched his head. He said something else in tailless talk. Then he started back toward the cub.

Torak watched Wolf's body tense.

Wolf's ears flicked forward. His black nose twitched.

Torak followed his gaze. He couldn't see anything through the tangle of hazel and willowherb, but he knew that the buck was in there, because Wolf knew it, and Torak had learned to trust Wolf.

Wolf glanced up at Torak, his amber eyes grazing the boy's. Then his gaze returned to the Forest.

Silently, Torak broke off a head of grass and split it with his thumbnail, letting the fine seeds float away on the breeze. Good. They were still downwind of the buck. It wouldn't catch their scent. And before setting out, Torak had, as always, masked his smell by smearing his skin with wood ash.

Without a sound, he drew an arrow from his quiver and fitted it to his bowstring. It was only a small roe buck, but if he could bring it down, it would be the first big kill he'd ever made on his own. He needed it. Prey was much scarcer than it should be at this time of year.

The cub's head sank low.

Torak crouched.

Together they crept forward.

They'd been tracking the buck all day. All day, Torak had followed its trail of bitten-off twigs and cloven prints, trying to feel what it was feeling, guessing where it would go next.

To track prey, you must first learn to know it as you would a brother. What it eats, and when and how; where it rests; how it moves. Fa had taught Torak well. He knew how to track. He knew that you must stop often to listen: to open your senses to what the Forest is telling you. . . .

Right now, he knew that the roe buck was tiring. Earlier in the day, the clefts of each small hoofprint had been deep and splayed, which meant it had been galloping. Now the clefts were lighter and closer together: It had slowed to a walk.

It must be hungry, because it hadn't had time to graze; and thirsty, because it had kept to the safety of the deep thickets, where there was no water.

Torak glanced about for signs of a stream. West through the hazel, about thirty paces off the trail, he glimpsed a clump of alders. Alders only grow near water. That was where the buck must be heading.

Softly, he and the cub moved through the undergrowth. Cupping his hand to his ear, he caught a faint ripple of water.

Suddenly, Wolf froze: ears rammed forward, one forepaw raised.

Yes. There. Through the alders. The buck stooping to drink.

Carefully Torak took aim.

The buck raised its head, water dripping from its muzzle.

Torak watched it snuff the air and fluff out its pale rump fur in alarm. Another heartbeat and it would be gone. He loosed his arrow.

It thudded into the buck's ribs just behind the shoulder. With a graceful shudder, the buck folded its knees and sank to the ground.

Torak gave a shout and pushed through the undergrowth toward it. Wolf raced him and easily won, but then pulled back to let Torak catch up. The cub was learning to respect the lead wolf.

Panting, Torak stood over the buck. Its ribs were still heaving, but death was near. Its three souls were getting ready to leave.

Torak swallowed. Now he had to do what he'd seen Fa do countless times. But for him it would be the first time, and he had to get it right.

Kneeling beside the buck, he put out his hand and gently stroked its rough, sweaty cheek. The buck lay quiet under his palm.

"You did well," Torak told it. His voice sounded awkward. "You were brave and clever, and you kept going all day. I promise to keep the pact with the World Spirit, and treat you with respect. Now go in peace."

He watched death glaze the great dark eye.

He felt grateful to the buck, but also proud. This was his first big kill. Wherever Fa was on the Death Journey, he would be pleased.

Torak turned to Wolf and put his head on one side, wrinkling his nose and baring his teeth in a wolf smile. *Well done; thank you.*

Wolf pounced on Torak, nearly knocking him over. Torak laughed and gave him a handful of blackberries from his food pouch. Wolf snuffled them up.

It had been seven days since they'd set out from the Fastwater, and still there was no sign of the bear. No tracks. No fur snagged on brambles. No more Forest-shaking roars.

Something was wrong, though. At this time of year, the Forest should be echoing with the bellows of rutting red deer, and the clash of their antlers as they fought for females. But all was silence. It was as if the Forest was slowly emptying, the prey fleeing from the unseen menace.

In seven days the only creatures Torak had encountered were birds and voles—and once, with heart-stopping suddenness, a hunting party: three men, two women, and a dog. Luckily, he'd managed to slip away before they saw him. *Stay away from men*, Fa had warned. *If they find out what you can do* . . .

Torak didn't know what that meant, but he knew Fa was right. He'd grown up away from people; he wanted nothing to do with them. Besides, he had Wolf now. With every day that passed, they understood each other better.

Torak was coming to know that wolf talk is a complex blend of gestures, looks, smells, and sounds. The gestures can be with the muzzle, ears, paws, tail, shoulders, fur, or the whole body. Many are very subtle: the merest tilt or twitch. Most do not involve sound. By now, Torak knew quite a lot of them, although it wasn't as if he'd had to learn them. It felt more as though he was remembering them.

Still, there was one thing he knew he'd never be able to master, because he wasn't a wolf. This was what he'd taken to calling "wolf sense": the cub's uncanny knack of sensing his thoughts and moods.

Wolf had his own moods, too. Sometimes he was the cub, with a puppyish love of berries and an inability to keep still—like the time he'd wriggled incessantly when Torak had held a naming rite for him, then licked off all the red alder juice daubed on his paws. Unlike Torak, who'd been nervous about performing so important a rite, Wolf had seemed unimpressed: merely impatient for it to be over.

At other times, though, he was the guide: mysteriously sure of the way they must take. But if Torak tried to ask him about that, he never gave much of an answer. *I just know.* That was all.

Right now, Wolf wasn't being the guide. He was being the cub. His muzzle was purple with blackberry juice, and he was yipping insistently for more.

Torak laughed and batted him away. "No more! I've got work to do."

Wolf shook himself, then went off to have a sleep.

It took Torak two full days to butcher the carcass. He'd made the buck a promise, and he had to keep it by not wasting a thing. That was the age-old pact between the hunters and the World Spirit. Hunters must treat prey with respect, and in return the Spirit would send more prey.

It was a daunting task. It takes many summers of practice to use prey well. Torak didn't make a very good job of it, but he did his best.

First, he slit the deer's belly and cut a slip of the liver for the clan guardian. The rest of the liver he cut into strips and set to dry. Then he relented and cut off a bit for Wolf, who slurped it up.

Next, Torak skinned the carcass, scraping the hide clean of flesh with his antler scraper. He washed the hide in water mixed with crumbled oak bark to loosen the hairs, then stretched it between two saplings—well out of Wolf's leaping range. Then he scraped off the hairs—inexpertly, making several holes—and softened the hide by rubbing it with mashed deer brain. After a final round of soaking and drying, he had a reasonable skin of rawhide for rope and fishing lines.

While the hide was drying, he cut the meat into thin strips and hung them over a smoky birchwood fire. When they were dry, he pounded them between two stones to make them thinner, then rolled them into small, tight bundles. The meat was delicious. One little piece would last him half a day.

The innards he washed, soaked in oak-bark water, and draped over a juniper bush to dry. The stomach would make a waterskin, the bladder a spare tinder pouch; the guts would store nuts. The lungs were Wolf's share—although not yet. Torak would chew them at daymeals and nightmeals, then spit them out for the cub. But as he had no cooking skin for making glue, he let Wolf have the hooves straightaway. The cub played with them tirelessly before crunching them to bits.

Next, Torak washed the long back sinews he'd saved from the butchering, pounded them flat, then teased out the narrow fibers for thread, drying them and rubbing them in fat to make them supple. They weren't nearly as smooth or even as the thread his father used to make, but they'd do. And they were so tough that they'd outlast any clothes he sewed with them.

Finally, he scraped the antlers and the long bones clean, and tied them into a bundle for splintering later into fishhooks, needles, and arrowheads.

It was late on the second day by the time he'd finished. He sat by the fire, pleasantly full of meat, whittling a whistle from a piece of grouse bone. He needed some way of summoning the cub when he was off on one of his solitary journeys, some way quieter than a howl. That hunting party might still be about. He couldn't risk any more howling.

He finished whittling and gave the whistle a try. To his dismay, it made no sound. Fa had carved countless whistles just like this one, and they'd always made a clear, birdlike chirp. Why didn't his?

Frustrated, Torak tried again, blowing as hard as he could. Still no sound. But to his surprise, Wolf leaped up as if he'd been stung by a hornet.

Torak glanced from the startled cub to the whistle. Once more he blew on it.

Again no sound. This time Wolf gave a brief snarl, then a whine, to show that he was a bit annoyed but didn't want to go too far and offend Torak.

Torak said he was sorry by gently scratching under Wolf's muzzle, and the cub slumped down. His expression made it clear: Torak shouldn't call unless he meant something by it.

Next day dawned fine and bright, and as they set off again, Torak's spirits rose.

It was twelve days since the bear had killed Fa. In that time Torak had fought hunger and conquered fever, found Wolf, and made his first big kill. He'd also made plenty of mistakes. But he was still alive.

He pictured his father on the journey to the Land of the Dead—the land where arrows are plentiful, and the hunt never fails. At least, thought Torak, he has his weapons with him, and my knife for company. And all that dried meat. That blunted the edge of his grief a little.

Torak knew that the loss of his father would never leave him—that he'd carry it in his chest all his life, like a stone. This morning the stone didn't feel quite so heavy. He'd survived so far, and his father would be proud.

He felt almost happy as he pushed through the undergrowth on the sun-dappled forest path. A couple of thrushes squabbled overhead. The fat, happy cub kept close to his side, his bushy silver tail held high.

Fat, happy, and careless.

Torak heard a twig snap behind him just as a large hand grabbed him by the jerkin and yanked him off his feet.

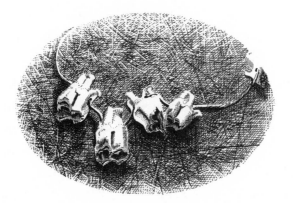

SEVEN

Three hunters. Three lethal flint weapons. All aimed at him.

Torak's mind whirled. He couldn't move. Couldn't see Wolf.

The man gripping his jerkin was enormous. His russet beard was a bird's-nest tangle; one cheek was pulled downward by an ugly scar, and whatever had bitten him had taken off one ear. In his free hand he held a flint-edged knife, its point jabbed under Torak's jaw.

Beside him stood a tall young man, and a girl about Torak's own age. Both had dark-red hair, smooth, pitiless faces, and flint arrows trained on his heart.

He tried to swallow. He hoped he didn't look as scared as he felt. "Let me go," he gasped. He took a swing at the big man and missed.

The big man grunted. "So here's our thief!" He hoisted Torak higher—chokingly high.

"I'm not—a thief!" coughed Torak, snatching at his throat.

"He's lying," the young man said coldly.

"You took our roe buck," said the girl. To the big man she said, "Oslak, I think you're choking him."

Oslak set Torak on his feet. But he didn't loosen his hold, and his knife stayed at Torak's throat.

Carefully, the girl replaced her arrow in her quiver and shouldered her bow. The young man did not. From the gleam in his eyes, it was clear that he was enjoying himself. He wouldn't hesitate to shoot.

Torak coughed and rubbed his throat, his other hand surreptitiously reaching for his knife.

"I'll take that," said Oslak. Still gripping Torak, he relieved him of his weapons and tossed them to the girl.

She studied Fa's knife curiously. "Did you steal this, too?"

"No!" said Torak. "It—it was my father's."

Clearly they didn't believe him.

Torak looked at the girl. "You said I took your buck. How could it be yours?"

"This is our part of the Forest," said the young man.

Torak was puzzled. "What do you mean? The Forest doesn't belong to anyone—"

"It does now," snapped the young man. "It was agreed at the clan meet. Because of—" He broke off with a scowl. "What matters is that you took our prey. That means death."

Torak broke out in a sweat. *Death?* How could taking a roe buck mean death?

His mouth was so dry that he could hardly speak. "If—if it's the buck you're after," he said, "take it and let me go. It's in my pack. I haven't eaten much."

Oslak and the girl exchanged glances, but the young man tossed his head in scorn. "It isn't that simple. You're my captive. Oslak, tie his hands. We're taking him to Fin-Kedinn."

"Where's that?" asked Torak as Oslak bound his hands behind his back with strips of rawhide.

"It's not a place," said Oslak. "It's a man."

"Don't you know anything?" sneered the girl.

"Fin-Kedinn is my uncle," said the young man, drawing himself up. "He's the Leader of our clan. I am Hord, his brother's son."

"What clan? Where are you taking me?"

They did not reply.

Oslak gave Torak a shove that knocked him to his knees. As he struggled to his feet, he glanced over his shoulder—and saw to his horror that Wolf had trotted back to look for him. He stood uncertainly some twenty paces away, snuffing the strangers' scent.

They hadn't spotted him. What would they do if they did? Presumably even they respected the ancient law that forbade the killing of another hunter. But what if they chased Wolf away? Torak pictured him lost in the Forest. Hungry. Howling.

To warn Wolf to stay out of sight, he gave a low, urgent "Uff." *Danger!*

Oslak nearly fell over him in surprise. "What did you say?"

"Uff!" said Torak again. To his dismay, Wolf didn't retreat. Instead, he put back his ears and raced straight for Torak.

"What's this?" muttered Oslak. He reached down and grabbed Wolf by the hackles.

Wolf wriggled and snarled as he dangled from the huge red hand.

"Let him go!" shouted Torak, struggling. "Let him go or I'll kill you!"

Oslak and the girl burst out laughing.

"Let him *go*! He's not doing you any harm!"

"Just chase it away and let's go," said Hord irritably.

"No!" yelled Torak. "He's my gui—no!"

The girl threw him a suspicious look. "He's your what?"

"He's with me," muttered Torak. He knew he mustn't reveal his search for the Mountain, or that he could talk to Wolf.

"Come on, Renn," snarled Hord. "We're wasting time."

But Renn was still staring at Torak. She turned to Oslak. "Give it to me." From her pack she pulled a buckskin bag into which she shoved the cub, drawing the neck tightly shut. As she shouldered the wriggling, yowling bag, she told Torak, "You'd better come quietly, or I'll bash him against a tree."

Torak glared at her. She probably wouldn't do it, but she'd just ensured his obedience far more effectively than either Oslak or Hord.

Oslak gave Torak another push, and they started along a deer track, heading northwest.

The rawhide bindings were tight, and Torak's wrists began to hurt. Well, let them, he thought. He was furious with himself. *Look behind you*, his father had said. He hadn't, and now he was paying for it—and so was Wolf. No more muffled yowls were coming from the bag. Was he suffocating? Already dead?

Torak begged Renn to open the bag and let in some air.

"No need," she said. "I just felt it wriggle."

Torak set his teeth and stumbled on. He had to find some way to escape.

Oslak was behind him, but Hord was right in front. He looked about nineteen, well built and handsome. He also seemed both arrogant and uneasy: desperate to be first, but scared that he'd only ever come second. His clothes were finely made and colorful, his jerkin and leggings stitched in braided sinew dyed red, and edged in some kind of bird skin stained green. On his chest he wore a magnificent necklace of red deer teeth.

Torak was mystified. Why would a hunter want so much color? And that necklace clinked, which was the last thing you needed.

Renn resembled Hord in feature, and Torak wondered if they were brother and sister, although Renn was younger by four or five summers. Her clan-tattoos—three fine blue-black bars on her cheekbones—showed clearly on her pale skin, giving her a sharp, mistrustful look. Torak didn't think he'd be asking her for help.

Her buckskin jerkin and leggings were scruffy, but her bow and quiver were beautiful, the arrows deftly fletched with owl feathers for silent flight. On the first two fingers of her left hand, she wore leather finger guards, and strapped to her right forearm was a wrist guard of polished green slate. Torak guessed that such wrist guards were worn by people who lived for their bows. That's what matters to her, he thought. Not fine clothes, like Hord.

But what clan was she? Sewn to the left side of her jerkin—and those of Hord and Oslak—was their clan-creature skin: a strip of black feathers. Swan? Eagle? The feathers were too tattered. Torak couldn't tell.

They walked all morning without stopping for food or water: crossing boggy valleys choked with chattering aspen; climbing hills darkened by ever-wakeful pines. As Torak passed beneath, the trees sighed mournfully, as if already lamenting his death.

Clouds obscured the sun, and he lost his bearings. They came to a slope where the Forest floor was bumpy with the waist-high nests of wood ants. As wood ants only build by the south side of trees, Torak worked out that they were heading west.

At last, they paused at a brook to drink.

"We're much too slow," growled Hord. "We've got a whole valley to cross before we reach the Windriver."

Torak pricked up his ears. Maybe he'd overhear something useful. . . .

Renn sensed he was listening. "The Windriver," she told him slowly, as if talking to a baby, "is to the west, in the next valley. It's where we camp in autumn. And a couple of daywalks to the north is the Widewater, where we camp in summer. For the salmon. They're fish. Maybe you've heard of them."

Torak felt himself reddening. But he knew now where they were heading: his captors' autumn camp. It sounded bad. A camp would mean more people, and less chance of escape.

As they walked, the sun sank lower, and Torak's captors became edgy, pausing often to listen and look about them. He guessed that they knew about the bear. Maybe that was why they'd adopted the unheard-of measure of "owning" prey. Because it was getting scarce; the bear was frightening it away.

They descended into a big valley of oak, ash, and pine, and soon reached a wide silver river. This must be the Windriver.

Suddenly Torak smelled woodsmoke. They were nearing the camp.

EIGHT

As the four of them crossed the river by a wooden walkway, Torak stared down at the sliding water and thought about jumping in. But his hands were tied. He'd drown. Besides, he couldn't leave Wolf.

About ten paces downstream, the trees opened into a clearing. Torak smelled pine smoke and fresh blood. He saw four big reindeer-hide shelters unlike any he'd ever seen, and a bewildering number of people: all hard at work, and as yet unaware of him. With a clarity born of fear, he took in every detail.

On the riverbank two men were skinning a boar strung from a tree. Having already slit the belly, they'd sheathed their knives and were peeling off the hide by hand, to avoid tearing it. Both were bare chested and wore fish-skin aprons over their leggings. They looked terrifyingly strong, with raised zigzag scars on their muscled arms. From the carcass, blood dripped slowly into a birch-bark pail.

In the shallows, two girls in buckskin tunics giggled as they rinsed the boar's guts, while three small children solemnly made mud cakes and studded them with sycamore wings. Two sleek hide canoes were drawn up out of the water. The ground around them glittered with fish scales. A couple of large dogs prowled for scraps.

In the middle of the clearing, near a pinewood long-fire, a group of women sat on willow-branch mats, talking quietly as they shelled hazelnuts and picked over a basket of juniper berries. None of them looked anything like Hord or Renn; Torak wondered briefly if, like him, they'd lost their parents.

A little apart from them, an old woman was heading arrows: slotting needle-fine flakes of flint into the shafts, then gluing them in place with a paste of pine-blood and beeswax. A round bone amulet etched with a spiral was sewn to the breast of her jerkin. From the amulet, Torak knew she must be the clan Mage. Fa had told him about Mages: people who can heal sickness, and dream where the prey is and what the weather will do. This old woman looked as if she could do far more dangerous things than that.

By the fire, a pretty girl leaned over a cooking skin. Steam crinkled her hair as she used a forked stick to drop in red-hot stones. The meaty smell of whatever was cooking made Torak's mouth water.

Near her, an older man knelt to spit a couple of hares. Like Hord, he had reddish-brown hair and a short red beard, but there the resemblance ended. His face had an arresting stillness, and a strength that made Torak think of carved sandstone. Torak forgot about the cooking smell. He knew, without being told, that this man wielded power.

Oslak untied the bindings and pushed Torak into the clearing. The dogs leaped up, barking ferociously. The old woman made a slicing motion with her palm, and they subsided into growls. Everyone stared at Torak. Everyone except the man by the fire, who went on calmly spitting the hares. Only when he'd finished did he rub off his hands in the dust and rise to his feet, waiting in silence for them to approach.

The pretty girl glanced at Hord and smiled shyly. "We saved you some broth," she said.

Torak guessed that either she was his mate or she wanted to be.

Renn turned and rolled her eyes at Hord. "Dyrati saved you some broth," she mocked.

Definitely his sister, thought Torak.

Hord ignored them both and went to talk to the man by the fire. Quickly, he related what had happened. Torak noticed that he made it sound as if he, not Oslak, had caught "the thief." Oslak didn't seem to mind, but Renn flashed her brother a sour glance.

Meanwhile, the dogs had scented Wolf. Hackles bristling, they advanced on Renn.

"Back!" she ordered. They obeyed. Renn ducked into the nearest shelter and emerged with a coil of wovenbark rope. She tied one end around the neck of the bag containing Wolf, tossed the other over the branch of an oak tree, and hoisted the bag high, well out of the dogs' reach.

And out of mine, realized Torak. Now even if he got the chance to escape, he couldn't. Not without Wolf.

Renn caught his eye and gave him a wry grin.

He scowled back. Inside, he was sick with fear.

Hord had finished talking. The man by the fire nodded once and waited for Oslak to push Torak toward him. His eyes were an intense, unblinking blue: vividly alive in that impenetrable face. Torak found it hard to look into them for long—and even harder to look away.

"What is your name?" said the man in a voice that was somehow more frightening for being so quiet.

Torak licked his lips. "Torak. What's yours?" But he

thought he already knew.

It was Hord who answered. "He is Fin-Kedinn. Leader of the Raven Clan. And you, you miserable little runt, should learn more respect—"

Fin-Kedinn silenced Hord with a look, then turned to Torak. "What clan are you?"

Torak raised his chin. "Wolf."

"Well, there's a surprise," remarked Renn, and several people laughed.

Fin-Kedinn wasn't one of them. His burning blue eyes never left Torak's face. "What are you doing in this part of the Forest?"

"Heading north," said Torak.

"I told him it belongs to us now," Hord put in quickly.

"How could I know that?" said Torak. "I wasn't at the clan meet."

"Why not?" said Fin-Kedinn.

Torak did not reply.

The Raven Leader's eyes drilled into his. "Where is the rest of your clan?"

"I don't know," said Torak truthfully. "I've never lived with them. I live—lived—with my father."

"Where is he?"

"Dead. He was—killed by a bear."

A hiss ran through the watchers. Some glanced fearfully over their shoulders; others touched their clan-creature skins, or made the sign of the hand to ward off evil. The old woman left her arrows and came toward them.

No emotion showed in Fin-Kedinn's face. "Who was your father?"

Torak swallowed. He knew—and so must Fin-Kedinn—that it is forbidden to speak a dead person's name for five summers after they die. Instead, they can only be referred to by naming their parents. Fa had hardly ever talked about his family, but Torak knew their names, and where they'd come from. Fa's mother had been Seal Clan; his father had been Wolf Clan. Torak named them both.

Recognition is one of the hardest expressions to conceal. Not even Fin-Kedinn could hide it completely.

He knew Fa, thought Torak, aghast. But how? Fa never mentioned him, or the Raven Clan. What does this mean?

He watched Fin-Kedinn run his thumb slowly across his bottom lip. It was impossible to tell whether Torak's father had been his best friend or his deadliest enemy.

At last Fin-Kedinn spoke. "Share out the boy's things among everyone," he told Oslak. "Then take him downstream and kill him."

NINE

Torak's knees buckled.

"Wh—at?" he gasped. "I didn't even know the buck was yours! How can I be guilty if I didn't know?"

"It's the law," said Fin-Kedinn.

"Why? *Why*? Because you say so?"

"Because the clans say so."

Oslak put a heavy hand on Torak's shoulder.

"No!" cried Torak. "Listen! You say it's the law, but—there's another law, isn't there?" He caught his breath. "Trial by combat. We—we fight for it." He wasn't sure if he'd got that right—Fa had only mentioned it once, when he was teaching him the law of the clans—but Fin-Kedinn's eyes narrowed.

"I'm right, aren't I?" Torak insisted, forcing himself to give the Raven Leader stare for stare. "You don't know for sure if I'm guilty, because you don't know whether I actually *knew* the buck was yours. So we fight. You and me." He swallowed. "If I win, I'm innocent. I live. I mean, me and the wolf. If I lose—we die."

Some of the men were chuckling. A woman tapped her brow, shaking her head.

"I don't fight boys," said Fin-Kedinn.

"But he's right, isn't he?" said Renn. "It's the oldest law of all. He has the right to fight."

Hord stepped forward. "I'll fight him. I'm closer to him in age. It'll be fairer."

"Not by much," Renn said drily.

She was leaning against the tree from which Wolf was suspended. Torak saw that she'd loosened the neck of the bag a little, so that Wolf's head was poking out. He looked bedraggled but was gazing curiously down at the two dogs slavering beneath him.

"What do you say, Fin-Kedinn?" said the Mage. "The boy's right. Let them fight."

Fin-Kedinn met the old woman's eyes, and for a moment there seemed to be a battle of wills between them. Slowly, he nodded.

Relief washed over Torak.

Everyone seemed to be excited by the prospect of a fight. They talked in huddles, stamping their feet, their breath steaming in the chill evening air.

Oslak tossed Torak his father's knife. "You'll need that. And a spear and an armguard."

"A what?" asked Torak.

The big man scratched the scar where his ear had been. "You know how to fight, don't you?"

"No," said Torak.

Oslak rolled his eyes. He went off to the nearest shelter, and returned with an ashwood spear tipped with a vicious basalt point and what seemed to be a length of triple-thickness reindeer hide.

Torak took the spear uncertainly, and watched in puzzlement as Oslak strapped the toughened hide around his right forearm for him. It felt as heavy and unwieldy as a haunch of deer meat. He wondered what he was supposed to do with it.

Oslak nodded at the bandage on Torak's other arm and grimaced. "Seems like the odds are against you."

Just a bit, thought Torak.

When he'd suggested a fight, he'd had in mind a wrestling bout, with maybe some knife play thrown in: the sort of thing he and Fa used to practice quite often, but just for fun. Clearly, to the Ravens, a fight meant something else. Torak wondered if there were special rules, and whether it would look weak to ask.

Fin-Kedinn prodded the fire, making sparks fly. Torak watched him through a shimmer of heat haze.

"There's only one rule," said Fin-Kedinn, as if he'd guessed Torak's thoughts. "You can't use fire. Do you understand?"

Torak nodded distractedly. Not using fire was the least of his worries. He could see Hord having his arm-guard strapped on behind Fin-Kedinn. He had taken off his jerkin. He looked enormous, and frighteningly strong. Torak decided against taking off his own jerkin. No need to emphasize the contrast.

He untied everything from his belt and laid it in a pile on the ground. Then he wound a length of woven-grass twine round his forehead to keep his hair out of his eyes. His hands were slippery with sweat. He stooped and rubbed them in the dust.

Someone touched his shoulder, making him jump.

It was Renn. She was holding out a birch-bark beaker.

He took it gratefully and drank. To his surprise, it was elderberry juice: tart and strengthening.

Renn saw his surprise and shrugged. "Hord's had a drink. It's only fair." She pointed to a pail by the fire. "There's water when you need it."

Torak handed back the beaker. "I don't think it'll last that long."

She hesitated. "Who knows?"

A hush fell. The watchers formed a ring round the edge of the clearing, with Torak and Hord in the middle, near the fire. There were no formalities. The fight was on.

Warily, they circled each other.

For all his size, Hord moved with the grace of a lynx, flexing his knees and repositioning his fingers on knife and spear. His face was taut, but a small smile played about his lips. He loved being the center of attention.

Torak didn't. His heart was hammering against his ribs. Dimly, he could hear the watchers shouting encouragement to Hord, but their voices were muffled, as if he were underwater.

Hord's spear lunged for his chest, and he dodged just in time. He felt the sweat start out on his forehead.

Torak tried the same move, hoping it didn't look like copying.

"Copying won't get you very far," called Renn.

Torak's face burned.

He and Hord were moving faster now. In places, the ground was slimy with boar's blood. Torak slipped and nearly went down.

He knew he couldn't hope to win by force. He'd have to use his wits. The trouble was, he only knew two fighting tricks, and he hadn't practiced them more than a few times.

Here goes, he thought recklessly. He jabbed his

spear at Hord's throat. As expected, Hord's hide-arm rose to block it. Torak tried a quick undercut to the belly, but Hord parried it with alarming ease, and Torak's spear slid harmlessly off his armguard.

He knew that one, thought Torak. With every move, it was becoming obvious that Hord was a seasoned fighter.

"Come on, Hord," yelled a man. "Give him a red skin!"

"Give me time," Hord called back with a curl of his lip.

A ripple of laughter.

Torak tried his second trick. Feigning total incompetence, which wasn't hard, he hit out wildly, tempting Hord with a glimpse of his unprotected chest. Hord took the bait, but as his spear came in to strike, Torak's guard arm swung across to meet it. Hord's spearpoint sank into the thick hide guard, nearly knocking Torak off his feet, but Torak managed to keep to his plan by twisting his arm sharply upward. Hord's spear-shaft snapped in two. The watchers groaned. Hord staggered back without a spear.

Torak was astonished. He hadn't expected it to work.

Hord recovered swiftly. Lunging forward, he jabbed his knife into Torak's spear-hand. Torak cried out as the flint bit between finger and thumb. He lost his footing and dropped his spear. Hord lunged again. Torak only just managed to roll away in time and scramble to his feet.

Now they were both spearless. Both down to knives.

To gain some breathing space, Torak dodged behind the fire. His chest was heaving, and his wounded hand throbbed. Sweat was pouring down his sides. He bitterly regretted not copying Hord and taking off his jerkin.

"Hurry up, Hord," yelled a woman. "Finish him off!"

"Come on, Hord!" shouted a man. "Is this what they taught you in the Deep Forest?"

By now, though, not all shouts were for Hord. There was a smattering of encouragement for Torak, although he guessed it was less genuine support than pleased surprise that he was lasting longer than expected.

He knew it wouldn't be much longer. He was tiring rapidly, and he'd run out of tricks. Hord was taking control.

Sorry, Wolf, he told the cub silently. I don't think we're going to get out of this.

From the corner of his eye, he glimpsed Wolf high in the tree. He was wriggling and yowling in a haze of steamy breath. *What's happening?* he was asking. *Why won't you come and free me?*

Torak leaped aside to avoid a knife slash across his throat. Concentrate, he told himself grimly. Forget about Wolf.

And yet—something was nagging him: something about Wolf. What was it?

He glanced at Wolf yowling in the tree, his breath steaming. . . .

"You can't use fire," Fin-Kedinn had said. . . .

Suddenly Torak knew what to do. Jabbing and feinting, he edged sideways, putting the fire between them once more.

"Hiding again?" taunted Hord.

Torak jerked his head at the birch-bark water pail. "I want a drink. All right?"

"If you must. *Boy.*"

Keeping his eyes on Hord, Torak squatted and cupped water to drink. He did it slowly, to make Hord think he was up to something with the water pail, and to distract attention from the cooking skin bubbling by the fire.

It worked. Hord stepped closer to the fire, looming over it to intimidate Torak.

"You want a drink too?" said Torak, still squatting.

Hord snorted his contempt.

Suddenly, Torak lashed out—but at the cooking-skin. Jabbing his knife into the tough hide, he upended it and sent boiling broth pouring onto the white-hot embers. Hissing clouds of steam billowed into Hord's face.

The watchers gasped. Torak seized his chance and jabbed at his opponent's wrist. Blinded, Hord howled in pain and dropped his knife. Torak kicked it away, then threw himself on Hord, knocking him to the ground.

As Hord lay winded, Torak straddled his chest and knelt on his arms to pin them down. For one roaring heartbeat his sight misted red, and he knew the urge to kill. He grabbed a handful of dark-red hair and bashed Hord's head once against the earth.

Then he felt strong hands on his shoulders, pulling him off. "It's over," said Fin-Kedinn behind him.

Torak struggled in his grip. Hord sprang up and scrambled for his knife. Panting and glaring, they faced each other.

"I said it's *over*," snapped Fin-Kedinn.

Chaos erupted among the watchers. They didn't think it was over at all. "He cheated! He used fire!"

"No, he won fairly enough!"

"Who's to say? They'll have to fight it out again!"

Both Torak and Hord looked appalled at that.

"The boy won," said Fin-Kedinn, releasing his grip on Torak.

Torak shook himself and wiped the sweat from his face as he watched Hord resheathing his knife. Hord was furious, though whether with himself or with Torak it was impossible to tell. Dyrati put her hand on his arm, but he shook it off angrily and pushed his way through the others, disappearing into one of the shelters.

Now that the blood lust had left him, Torak felt shaky and sick. He sheathed his knife and looked around for his things. Then he saw Fin-Kedinn watching him.

"You broke the rule," the Raven Leader said calmly. "You used fire."

"No I didn't," said Torak. He sounded a lot more confident than he felt. "I didn't use fire. I used steam."

"I would have preferred it," said Fin-Kedinn, "if you'd used water instead of broth. That was a waste of good food."

Torak did not reply.

Fin-Kedinn studied him, and for a moment there was a gleam of humor in his blue eyes.

Oslak pushed through to them, with the bag containing Wolf in his arms. "Here's that cub of yours!" he boomed, tossing the bag at Torak with a force that made him stagger.

Wolf squirmed and licked Torak's chin and told him how awful it had been, all at once. Torak wanted to say something comforting but stopped himself. It would be stupid to slip up now.

"The law's the law," Fin-Kedinn said briskly. "You won. You're free to go."

"No!" A girl's voice rang out, and all heads turned. It was Renn. "You can't let him go!" she cried, running forward.

"He just has," retorted Torak. "You heard him. I'm free."

Renn spoke to her uncle. "We can't let him go. This is too important. He might be . . ." She drew Fin-Kedinn aside, whispering urgently.

Torak couldn't make out what she was saying, but to his dismay, others drew closer to listen. The Mage scowled and nodded. Even Hord emerged from the shelter, and when he heard what they were saying, he gave Torak a strange, wary stare.

Fin-Kedinn studied Renn thoughtfully. "Are you sure about this?"

"I don't *know*," she said. "Maybe he is. Maybe he isn't. We need time to find out."

Fin-Kedinn stroked his beard. "What makes you suspect—"

"The way he defeated Hord. And I found this in his things." She held out her palm, and Torak saw his little grouse-bone whistle. "What do you use it for?" she asked him.

"For calling the cub," he replied.

She blew on it, and Wolf twisted in his arms. A

shiver of unease ran through the crowd. Renn and Fin-Kedinn exchanged glances. "It doesn't make any noise," she said accusingly.

Torak did not reply. He realized with a jolt that her eyes were not light blue like her brother's, but black: black as a peat pool. He wondered if she was a Mage, too.

She turned to Fin-Kedinn. "We can't let him go till we know for sure."

"She's right," said the Mage. "You know what it says as well as I do. Everyone does."

"What *what* says?" pleaded Torak. "Fin-Kedinn, we had a pact! We agreed that if I won the fight, me and Wolf would go free!"

"No," said Fin-Kedinn, "we agreed that you would live. And so you shall. At least for now. Oslak, tie him up again."

"*No!*" shouted Torak.

Renn raised her chin. "You said your father was killed by a bear. We know about that bear. Some of us have even seen it."

Beside her, Hord shuddered and began to gnaw his thumbnail.

"About a moon ago it came," Renn went on quietly. "Like a shadow it darkened the Forest, killing wantonly, even killing other hunters. Wolves. A lynx. It was as if—as if it was searching for something." She paused. "Then thirteen days ago it disappeared. A runner from the Boar Clan tracked it south. We thought it had gone. We gave thanks to our clan guardian." She swallowed. "Now it's back. Yesterday our scouts returned from the west. They'd found many kills, right down to the Sea. The Whale Clan told them that three days ago, it took a child."

Torak licked his lips. "What's this got to do with me?"

"There's a Prophecy in our clan," said Renn as if he hadn't spoken. "*A Shadow attacks the Forest. None can stand against it.*'" She broke off, frowning.

The Mage took up her words. "'*Then comes the Listener. He fights with air, and speaks with silence.*'" Her gaze fell on the whistle in Renn's hand.

Everyone was silent, watching Torak.

"I'm not your Listener," he said.

"We think you might be," replied the Mage.

Torak thought about the Prophecy. "*The Listener fights with air. . . .*" He had done just that: He had used steam. "What—happens to him?" he asked in a low voice. "What happens to the Listener in the Prophecy?" But he had a terrible feeling that he already knew.

The silence in the clearing grew more intense. Torak looked from the frightened faces around him to the flint knife at Oslak's belt. He looked at the glistening carcass of the boar hanging from the tree; at its dark blood trickling into the pail beneath. He felt Fin-Kedinn's eyes on him and turned to face the burning blue gaze.

"*The Listener,*'" quoted Fin-Kedinn, "'*gives his heart's blood to the Mountain. And the Shadow is crushed.*'"

His heart's blood.

Under the tree, the blood dripped softly into the pail.

Drip, drip, drip.

TEN

"What are you going to do to me?" asked Torak as Oslak tied his wrists behind his back and then to the roof post. "What are you going to do?"

"You'll know soon enough," said Oslak. "Fin-Kedinn wants it settled by dawn."

Dawn, thought Torak.

Over his shoulder, he watched Oslak tying a reluctant Wolf to the same roof post on a short rawhide leash.

His teeth began to chatter. "Who decides what happens to me? Why can't I be there to defend myself? Who are all those people by the fire?"

"Ow!" exclaimed Oslak, sucking a bitten finger. "Fin-Kedinn sent runners to call a clan meet about the bear. Now they're deciding about you, too."

Torak peered at the figures hunched about the long-fire: twenty or thirty men and women, their faces starkly lit by the flames. He didn't give much for his chances.

Dawn. Somehow, before dawn, he had to get out of here.

But how? He was sitting in a shelter, tied to a roof post, without weapons or pack; and even if he got free, the camp was heavily guarded. Now that darkness had fallen, a ring of fires had sprung up around it, and men with spears and birch-bark horns were keeping watch. Fin-Kedinn was taking no chances with the bear.

Oslak yanked off Torak's boots and tied his ankles together, then left, taking the boots with him.

Torak couldn't hear what they were saying at the clan meet, but at least he could see them, thanks to the odd construction of the Raven shelter. Its reindeer-hide roof sloped sharply down behind him, but in front there was no wall at all, only a crossbeam, which seemed to deflect the smoke from the small fire that crackled just in front but trapped the warmth inside.

Straining to make out what was going on, Torak saw people rising one by one to speak. A broad-shouldered man holding an enormous throwing axe. A woman with long nut-brown hair, one lock at the temple matted with red ochre. A wild-eyed girl whose skull was weirdly plastered with yellow clay to give it the roughness of oak bark.

He couldn't see Fin-Kedinn, but a little apart from the others, the Mage crouched in the dust, watching a large glossy raven. The bird stalked fearlessly up and down, uttering the occasional harsh *"cark!"*

Torak wondered if it was the clan guardian. What was it telling her? How to sacrifice him? Whether to gut him like a salmon or spit him like a hare? He'd never heard of clans sacrificing people, except long in the past, in the bad times after the Great Wave. But then, he'd never heard of the Raven Clan either.

Fin-Kedinn wants it decided by dawn. . . . The Listener gives his heart's blood to the Mountain. . . .

Had Fa known about the Prophecy? He couldn't have. He wouldn't have sent his own son to his death.

And yet—he'd made Torak swear to find the Mountain. He'd said, *Don't hate me later.*

Later. When you find out.

The cub's rasping tongue on his wrists brought him back to the present. Wolf liked the taste of the rawhide. Torak felt a surge of hope. If Wolf could be made to bite instead of lick . . .

Even as Torak was wondering how to put that in wolf talk, a man rose from the long-fire and crossed the clearing toward him. It was Hord.

Frantically, Torak growled at Wolf to stop. He was too hungry to notice, and went on licking.

Hord wasn't interested in Wolf, though. He stood by the smaller fire in front of the doorway, gnawing his thumbnail and glaring at Torak. "You're not the Listener," he snarled. "You can't be."

"Tell that to the others," retorted Torak.

"We don't need a *boy* to help us kill the bear. We can do it ourselves. *I* can do it. I'll save the clans."

"You wouldn't stand a chance," said Torak. He felt Wolf starting to nibble the rawhide with his sharp front teeth, and kept very still so as not to put him off. He prayed that Hord wouldn't look behind him and see what Wolf was doing.

But Hord seemed too agitated to notice. He paced back and forth, then turned on Torak. "You've seen it, haven't you? You've seen the bear."

Torak was startled. "Of course I've seen it. It killed my father."

Hord cast a furtive glance over his shoulder. "I've seen it too."

"Where? When?"

Hord flinched, as if warding off a blow. "I was in the south. With the Red Deer Clan. I was learning Magecraft. Saeunn"—he nodded at the old woman talking to the raven—"our Mage, she wanted me to go." Again he tore at his thumbnail, which had started to bleed. "I was there when the bear was caught. I—I saw it made."

Torak stared at him. "Made? What do you mean?"

But Hord had gone.

Middle-night passed, the dying moon rose, and still the clan meet went on. Still Wolf licked and nibbled at the rawhide. But Oslak had tied the knots securely, and Wolf couldn't seem to get his jaws around them. Don't stop, Torak begged him silently. *Please* don't stop.

He was too scared to be hungry, but he felt bruised and stiff from the fight with Hord, and his shoulders ached from being tied up for so long. Even if Wolf managed to gnaw through the bindings, he wasn't sure that he'd have the strength to run away, or slip between the guards.

He kept thinking about what Hord had said. "I saw it made. . . ."

There was something else, too. Hord had been with the Red Deer Clan, and Torak's mother had been Red Deer. He'd never known her—she'd died when he was little; but if the Ravens were friendly with her clan, then maybe he could persuade them to let him go. . . .

Outside, boots scuffed the dust. Quick. They mustn't catch Wolf at his wrists.

Torak just had time for a swift warning "Uff!"—

which luckily Wolf obeyed—before Renn appeared in the doorway, chewing a leg of roast hare.

Her sharp eyes took in Wolf sitting innocently behind him, then fixed on Torak—who stared back, willing her not to come any closer.

He jerked his head at the clan meet and asked if any Wolf Clan were present.

She shook her head. "Not many Wolf Clan left these days. So you're not going to be rescued, if that's what you're thinking."

Torak did not reply. He'd just pulled at the rope around his wrists and felt it give a little. It was beginning to stretch, as rawhide does when it gets wet. If only Renn would go away.

She stayed exactly where she was. "No Wolf Clan," she said with her mouth full, "but plenty of others. Yellow Clayhead over there is from the Auroch Clan. They're Deep Forest people; they pray a lot. That's how they think we should deal with the bear, by praying to the World Spirit. The man with the axe is Boar Clan. He wants to make a fire wall to drive the bear toward the Sea. The woman with the earthblood in her hair is Red Deer. Not sure what she thinks. With them it's hard to tell."

Torak wondered why she was talking so much. What did she want?

Whatever it was, he decided to go along with it. He

said, "My mother was Red Deer. Maybe that woman over there is my bone kin. Maybe—"

"She says not. She's not going to help you."

He thought for a moment. "Your clan are friendly with the Red Deer, aren't they? Your brother said he learned Magecraft with them."

"So?"

"He—he told me he saw the bear 'made.' What did he mean?"

She gave him her narrow, mistrustful stare.

"I need to know," said Torak. "It killed my father."

Renn studied the hare's leg. "Hord was fostered with them. You know about fostering, don't you?" Her voice held a touch of scorn. "It's when you stay with another clan for a while; to make friends, and maybe find a mate."

"I've heard of it," said Torak. Behind him, he felt Wolf snuffling at his wrists again. He tried to bat him away with his fingers, but it didn't work. Not now, he thought. Please not now.

"He was with them for nine moons," said Renn, taking another bite of the hare leg. "They're the best at Magecraft in the Forest. That's why he went." Her mouth curled humorlessly. "Hord likes to be the best." Then she frowned. "What's that cub doing?"

"Nothing," Torak said too quickly. To Wolf he said in a stilted voice, "Go away. Go away."

Wolf, of course, ignored him.

Torak turned back to Renn. "What happened next?"

Another look. "Why are you asking?"

"Why are you talking to me?"

Her face closed. She was as good at keeping things back as Fin-Kedinn.

Thoughtfully she picked a shred of hare from between her teeth. "Hord hadn't been with the Red Deer long," she said, "when a stranger came to their camp. A wanderer from the Willow Clan, crippled by a hunting accident. Or so he said. The Red Deer took him in. But he—" She hesitated, and suddenly looked younger and much less confident. "He betrayed them. He wasn't just a wanderer; he knew Magecraft. He made a secret place in the woods and conjured a demon. Trapped it in the body of a bear." She paused. "Hord found out. By then it was too late."

Beyond the shelter, the shadows seemed to have deepened. Out in the Forest, a fox screamed.

"*Why?*" said Torak. "Why did he do it, this— wanderer?"

Renn shook her head. "Who knows? Maybe to have a creature to do his bidding? But it went wrong." The firelight glinted in her dark eyes. "Once the demon got inside the bear, it was too strong. It broke free. Killed three people before the Red Deer could drive it away.

By then the crippled wanderer had disappeared."

Torak was silent. The only sounds were the trees whispering in the night breeze, and the rasp of Wolf's tongue as he licked the rawhide.

Wolf accidentally caught Torak's skin in his teeth. Without thinking, Torak turned and gave him a sharp warning growl.

Instantly Wolf leaped back and apologized with a grin.

Renn gasped. "You can *talk* to him!"

"No!" cried Torak. "No, you're wrong—"

"I *saw* you!" Her face was paler than ever. "So it's true. The Prophecy is true. You *are* the Listener."

"No!"

"What were you saying to him? What were you plotting?"

"I've told you, I can't—"

"I won't give you the chance," she whispered. "I won't let you plot against us. Neither will Fin-Kedinn." Drawing her knife, she cut Wolf's leash, scooped him up in her arms, and raced across the clearing toward the clan meet.

"Come back!" yelled Torak. Furiously, he yanked at the bindings, but they held fast. Wolf hadn't had time to bite them through.

Terror washed over him. He'd put all his hopes in Wolf, and now Wolf was gone. Dawn was not far off.

Already the birds were stirring in the trees.

Again he tugged at the bindings around his wrists. Again they held tight.

Across the clearing, Fin-Kedinn and the old woman called Saeunn rose to their feet and started toward him.

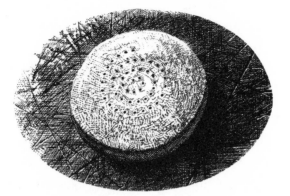

ELEVEN

"How much do you know?" said Fin-Kedinn.

"Nothing," said Torak, eyeing the jagged bone knife at the Raven Leader's belt. "Are you going to sacrifice me?"

Fin-Kedinn did not reply. He and Saeunn crouched at either side of the doorway, watching him. He felt like prey.

Behind his back, he scrabbled around for something—anything—that he could use to cut the rawhide. His fingers found only a willow-branch mat: smooth and useless.

"How much do you know?" Fin-Kedinn said again.

Torak took a deep breath. "I am not your Listener," he said as steadily as he could. "I can't be. I've never even heard of the Prophecy." And yet, he wondered, why was Renn so certain? What does speaking wolf talk have to do with it?

Fin-Kedinn turned away. His face was as unreadable as ever, but Torak saw his hand tighten on his knife.

Saeunn leaned forward and peered into Torak's eyes. In the firelight, he saw her closely. He'd never encountered anyone so old. Through her scant white hair, her scalp gleamed like polished bone. Her face was sharp as a bird's. Age had scorched away all kindly feelings to leave only the fierce raven essence.

"According to Renn," she said harshly, "you can talk to the wolf. That's part of the Prophecy. The part we didn't tell you."

"Renn's wrong," Torak said quickly. "I can't—"

"Don't lie to us," said Fin-Kedinn without turning his head.

Torak swallowed.

Again he groped behind him. This time—yes! A tiny flake of flint, no bigger than his thumbnail: probably dropped by someone sharpening a knife. His fingers closed over it. If only Fin-Kedinn and Saeunn would return to the clan meet, he might be able to cut himself free. Then he could find wherever Renn had taken Wolf, and dodge between the guards and . . .

His spirits sank. He'd need a lot of luck to manage all that.

"Shall I tell you," said Saeunn, "*why* you can talk to the wolf?"

"Saeunn, what's the use?" said Fin-Kedinn. "We're wasting time—"

"He must be told," said the old woman. She fell silent. Then, with one yellow, clawlike finger, she touched the amulet at her breast and began tracing the spiral.

Torak watched her talon going round and round. He started to feel dizzy.

"Many years ago," said the Raven Mage, "your father and mother left their clan. They went to hide from their enemies. Far, far away in the Deep Forest, among the green souls of the talking trees." Still her talon traced the spiral: drawing Torak down into the past.

"Three moons after you were born," Saeunn went on, "your mother died."

Fin-Kedinn got up, crossed his arms over his chest, and stood staring out into the darkness.

Saeunn didn't even glance at Fin-Kedinn. Her attention was fixed on Torak. "You were only an infant," she said. "Your father couldn't feed you. Usually when that happens, the father smothers his child, to spare it a slow death from starvation. But your father found another way. A she-wolf with a litter. He put you in her den."

Torak struggled to take it in.

"Three moons you were with her in the den. Three moons to learn the wolf talk."

Torak gripped the flint flake so hard that it dug into his palm. He could feel that Saeunn was telling the truth. This was why he could talk to Wolf. This was why he'd had that vision when he'd found the den. The squirming cubs. The rich, fatty milk . . .

How could Saeunn possibly know?

"No," he said. "This is a trap. You couldn't know this. You weren't there."

"Your father told me," said Saeunn.

"He can't have. We never went near people—"

"Oh, but you did once. Five summers ago. Don't you remember? The clan meet by the Sea."

Torak's pulse began to race.

"Your father went there to find me. To tell me about you." Her talon came to rest at the heart of the spiral. "You are not like others," she said in her raven's croak. "You *are* the Listener."

Again Torak's grip on the flint tightened. "I—I can't be. I don't understand."

"Of course he doesn't," said Fin-Kedinn over his shoulder. He turned to Torak. "Your father told you nothing about who you are. That's right, isn't it?"

Torak nodded.

The Raven Leader was silent for a moment. His face was still, but Torak sensed a battle raging beneath his masklike features. "There is only one thing you need to know," said Fin-Kedinn. "It's this. It is not by chance that the bear attacked your father. It's *because* of him that it came into being."

Torak's heart missed a beat. "Because of my father?"

"Fin-Kedinn—" warned Saeunn.

The Raven Leader shot her a sharp glance. "You said he should know. Now I'm telling him."

"But," said Torak, "it was the crippled wanderer who—"

"The crippled wanderer," cut in Fin-Kedinn, "was your father's sworn enemy."

Torak shrank back against the roof post. "My father didn't have enemies."

The Raven Leader's eyes glinted dangerously. "Your father wasn't just some hunter from the Wolf Clan. He was the Wolf Clan Mage."

Torak forgot to breathe.

"He didn't tell you that, either, did he?" said Fin-Kedinn. "Oh yes, he was the Wolf Mage. And it's because of him that this—*creature*—is rampaging through the Forest—"

"No," whispered Torak. "That isn't true."

"He kept you ignorant of everything, didn't he?"

"Fin-Kedinn," said Saeunn, "he was trying to protect—"

"Yes, and look at the result!" Fin-Kedinn rounded on her. "A half-grown boy who knows nothing! Yet you ask me to believe that he is the only one who can—" He stopped short, shaking his head.

There was a taut silence. Fin-Kedinn took a deep breath. "The man who created the bear," he told Torak quietly, "did it for a single purpose. He created the bear to kill your father."

The sky was lightening in the east when Torak finally cut the rope round his wrists with the flake of flint. There was no time to lose. Fin-Kedinn had just gone back to the clan meet with Saeunn, where they were locked in heated argument with the others. At any moment they might reach a decision and come to get him.

It was an effort to saw through the binding at his ankles. His head was reeling. *Your father put you in the den of a she-wolf. . . . He was the Wolf Mage. . . . He was murdered. . . .*

The flake of flint was slippery with sweat. He dropped it. Fumbled for it again. At last the binding was cut. He flexed his ankles—and nearly cried out in pain. His legs burned from being cramped for so long.

Worse than that was the pain in his heart. Fa had been murdered. Murdered by the crippled wanderer, who had created the demon bear with the sole aim of hunting him down. . . .

It wasn't possible. There had to be some mistake.

And yet, deep down, Torak knew it was true. He remembered the grimness in Fa's face as he lay dying. *It will come for me soon*, he had said. He had known what his enemy had done. He had known why the bear had been created.

It was too much to take in. Torak felt as if everything he'd ever known had been swept away, as if he stood on day-old ice, watching the cracks spreading like lightning beneath his feet.

The pain in his legs wrenched him back to the present. He tried to rub some feeling into them. His bare feet were cold, but there was nothing he could do. He hadn't been able to see where Oslak had taken his boots.

Somehow, without being spotted, he had to get out of the shelter, across to the hazel bushes at the edge of the clearing. Somehow, he had to evade the guards.

He couldn't do it. He'd be seen. If only he could find some way to distract them . . .

At the far end of the camp, a lonely yowl rose into the misty morning air. *Where are you?* cried Wolf. *Why did you leave me this time?*

Torak froze. He heard the camp dogs taking up the howl. He saw people leaping up from the clan meet and running to investigate. He knew that Wolf had given him his chance.

He had to act fast. Quickly, he edged out of the shelter and dived into the shadows behind the hazel bushes. He knew what he had to do—and he hated it.

He had to leave Wolf behind.

TWELVE

Cold air burned Torak's throat as he tore through a willow thicket toward the river. Stones bloodied his bare feet. He hardly noticed.

Thanks to Wolf, he'd gotten out of the camp unseen, but not for long. Behind him came a deep, echoing boom. Birch-bark horns were sounding the alarm. He heard men shouting, dogs baying. The Ravens were coming after him.

Brambles snagged his leggings as he skidded over the riverbank and splashed down into a bed of tall reeds. Knee-deep in icy black mud, he clamped his hand over his mouth to stop his steamy breath from betraying him.

Fortunately, he was downwind of his pursuers, but the sweat was pouring off him, and he was still clutching the rawhide rope from his ankles; the dogs would easily pick up his scent. He didn't know whether to toss it away or keep it in case he needed it.

Confusion swirled in his head like an angry river. He had no boots, no pack, no weapons—and nothing with which to make any more, apart from the knowledge in his head and the skill in his hands. If he managed to escape, what then?

Suddenly, above the horns, he heard a yowl. *Where are you?*

At the sound, Torak's doubts cleared. He couldn't leave Wolf. He had to rescue him.

He wished there was some way he could howl back—*I'm coming. Don't be afraid, I haven't abandoned you*—but of course there wasn't. The yowling went on.

His feet were freezing. He had to get out of the river or he'd be too numb to run. He thought fast.

The Ravens would expect him to head north, because that was where he'd said he was going when they'd captured him; so he decided to do exactly that— at least for a while—and then double back to the camp and find some way of reaching Wolf, hoping that the Ravens would be tricked into continuing north.

Farther downstream, a branch snapped.

Torak wheeled round.

A soft splash. A muttered curse.

He peered through the reeds.

About fifty paces downstream, two men were stealing down the bank toward the reed bed. They moved carefully, intent on hunting him. One held a bow that was taller than Torak, with an arrow already fitted to the string; the other gripped a basalt throwing axe.

It had been a mistake to hide in the reed bed. If he stayed where he was, they'd find him; if he tried to swim the river, he'd be seen and speared like a pike. He had to get back into the cover of the Forest.

As quietly as he could, he started clambering up the bank. It was thick with willows that gave good cover, but very steep. Red earth crumbled beneath him. If he fell back into the river, they'd hear the splash. . . .

Pebbles trickled into the water as he clawed at the dirt. Luckily the booming of the birch-bark horns masked the noise, and the men didn't hear.

Chest heaving, he made it to the top. Now to head north. The sky was overcast, so he couldn't get his bearings from the sun, but since the river flowed west, he knew that if he kept it directly behind him, he'd be heading roughly north.

He set off through a thick wood of aspen and beech, taking care to trail the rawhide behind him so as to leave a good strong scent.

A furious baying erupted behind him, terrifyingly

close. He'd trailed the rope too soon. Already the dogs had picked up his scent.

In panic he scrambled up the nearest tree—a spindly aspen—and had just managed to screw the rawhide into a ball and throw it as far as he could toward the river when a massive red dog burst through the brambles.

It cast about beneath Torak's tree, loops of spit swinging from its jaws. Then it picked up the scent of the rawhide and raced off in pursuit.

"There!" came a shout from downstream. "One of the dogs has found the trail!"

Three men ran beneath Torak's aspen, panting as they struggled to catch up with the dog. Torak clung to the tree trunk. If one of them looked up . . .

They pushed on and disappeared. Moments later, Torak heard faint splashes. They must be searching the reeds.

He waited in case more followed, then jumped down from the tree.

He ran north through the aspens, putting some distance between himself and the river, then skidded to a halt. It was time to turn east and head back toward the camp—provided he could find some way of putting the dogs off his trail.

Desperately he looked around for something to mask his scent. Deer droppings? No good: the dogs would still chase after him. Yarrow leaves? Maybe. Their strong, nutty smell should be powerful enough to mask his sweat.

At the foot of a beech tree, he found a pile of wolverine droppings: twisted, hairy, and so foul-smelling that they made his eyes water. Much better. Gagging on the stench, he smeared his feet, shins, and hands. Wolverines are about the same size as badgers, but they'll fight anything that moves, and they usually win. The dogs probably wouldn't risk an encounter.

The booming of the horns suddenly cut off.

The silence beat at his ears. With a clutch of terror he realized that Wolf's yowls had also ceased. Was he all right? Surely—surely the Ravens wouldn't dare harm him?

Torak fought his way through the undergrowth toward the camp. The ground rose, and the river ran swiftly between tumbled boulders slippery with moss.

Ahead, smoke curled into the heavy gray sky. He must be getting close. He crouched, straining for sounds of pursuit above the rushing water. With every breath, he expected to hear the thwang of a bowstring; to feel an arrow slicing between his shoulder blades.

Nothing. Maybe they'd fallen for his trick and were following his trail north.

Through the trees, something big and domed rose into sight. Torak lurched to a halt. He guessed what it was, and hoped he was wrong.

Like a huge toad, the mound squatted above him. It was a head taller than him, and thickly covered with moss and blueberry scrub. Behind it stood two smaller mounds, and around them loomed a dense thicket of yews and ivy-choked holly trees.

Torak hung back, wondering what to do. Once, he and Fa had come across mounds like these. This was the Raven Clan's bone-ground: the place where they laid the bones of their Dead.

His way to the camp—to Wolf—lay through the bone-ground. But would he dare? He wasn't Raven Clan. He couldn't venture into another clan's bone-ground without angering their ancestors. . . .

Mist floated in the hollows between the mounds, where the pale, ghostly skeletons of hemlock reared above his head and the purple stalks of dying willow-herb released their eerily drifting down. All around stood the dark, listening trees: trees that stayed green all winter, that never slept. In the branches of the tallest yew perched three ravens, watching him. He wondered which one was the clan guardian.

A baying of dogs behind him.

He was caught in a trap. Clever Fin-Kedinn: throwing his net wide, then tightening it around the quarry.

Torak had nowhere to go. The river was too fast to swim, and if he climbed a tree, the ravens would tell the hunters where he was, and he'd be dropped like a shot squirrel. If he burrowed into the thicket, the dogs would drag him out like a weasel.

He turned to face his pursuers. He had nothing with which to defend himself; not even a rock.

He edged backward—straight into the largest mound. He stifled a cry. He was caught between the living and the Dead.

Something grabbed him from behind and dragged him down into darkness.

THIRTEEN

"Don't move," breathed a voice in Torak's ear, "don't make a sound, and *don't touch the bones*!"

Torak couldn't even see the bones; he couldn't see anything. He was huddled in rotten-smelling blackness with a knife pressed to his throat.

He gritted his teeth to stop them from chattering. Around him, he sensed the chill weight of earth and the massed and moldering bones of the Raven Dead. He prayed that all the souls would be far away on the Death Journey. But what if some had been left behind?

In the first shock of being caught, he'd heard a scraping of stone, as if his captor was sealing the mound. Now, as his eyes adjusted to the dark, he made out a faint edge of light. Whatever had been dragged across the entrance didn't seem to be a perfect fit.

He was thinking about making a run for it when he heard voices outside. Faint, but coming closer.

Torak tensed. So did his captor.

The crunch and rustle drew nearer, then halted about three paces away. "He'd never dare come here," said a man's hushed, frightened voice.

"He might," whispered a woman. "He's different. You saw the way he won against Hord. Who knows what he'd do?"

Torak heard the squelch of moss. His foot twitched—and in the darkness, something clinked. He winced.

"Sh!" said the woman. "I heard something!"

Torak held his breath. His captor's knife pressed harder.

Cark! A raven's cry echoed through the trees.

"The guardian doesn't want us here," muttered the woman. "We should go. You're right. The boy wouldn't dare."

Sick with relief, Torak listened to them move away.

After a while he tried to shift position, but the knife point stopped him. "Stay still!" hissed his captor.

He recognized that voice. It was Renn. *Renn?*

"You stink," she whispered.

He tried to turn his head, but again the knife stopped him. "It's to keep the dogs away," he whispered back.

"They'd never come here anyway, they're not allowed."

Torak thought for a moment. "How did you know I'd be coming this way? And why—"

"I didn't. Now be quiet. They might come back."

After a cold, cramped wait that seemed to last forever, Renn gave him a kick and told him to move. He thought about trying to overpower her, but decided against it. If there was a struggle, they would disturb the bones. Instead, he heaved aside the slate slab that blocked the entrance and crawled into the daylight. The mounds were deserted. Even the ravens had gone.

Renn came after him, backing out on hands and knees and dragging two hazelwood packs—one of them his own. Perplexed, he crouched in the willow-herb and watched her go back inside, emerging with two rolled up sleeping-sacks, two quivers and bows—both wrapped in salmon skin against the damp—and a buckskin bag that was wriggling furiously.

"Wolf!" cried Torak.

"*Quiet!*" Renn darted a wary glance in the direction of the camp.

Torak wrenched open the bag and Wolf shot out, sweaty and bedraggled. He took one sniff and would have fled if Torak hadn't grabbed him and assured him in low half barks that it really was him and not some murderous wolverine. Wolf broke into a big wolf-smile, wagging his hindquarters and nibble-greeting Torak rapturously under the chin.

"Hurry up," said Renn behind him.

"Coming," snapped Torak. Grabbing handfuls of dew-soaked moss, he wiped off the worst of the dung, then yanked on his boots. Renn had had the foresight to bring them, too.

As he turned to reach for his pack, he saw to his astonishment that she had fitted an arrow to her bow and was training it on him. She'd also slung his own bow and quiver over her shoulder and stuck his axe and knife in her belt.

"What are you doing?" he said. "I thought you were helping me."

She looked at him in disgust. "Why would I help you? The only thing I'm helping is my clan."

"Then why didn't you give me away just now?"

"Because I intend to make sure that you get to the Mountain of the World Spirit. If I didn't make you, you wouldn't even try. You'd just turn tail and run. Because you're a coward."

Torak gasped. "A *coward*?"

"A coward, a liar, and a thief. You stole our roe buck, you tricked Hord into losing the fight, and you lied about not being the Listener. Then you ran away. Now for the last time, move!"

With Renn's arrow at his back and her accusation burning in his ears, Torak headed west downriver, keeping to the willows for cover, and carrying Wolf in his arms to prevent his pads leaving a scent trail for the dogs.

Amazingly, there were no sounds of pursuit. Torak found that even more disturbing than the birch-bark horns.

Renn set a fast pace, and he stumbled often. He was tired and hungry, while she was rested and fed; that would make getting away from her more difficult. But she was smaller than him, and he thought he could probably overpower her before she did too much damage with that bow.

The question was, when? For the moment, she seemed genuinely eager to evade the Ravens, guiding him along little twisting deer paths that clung to the best cover. He decided to wait till they were farther from the camp. But her insult rankled.

"I'm not a coward," he said over his shoulder, as they followed the river into a shady oak wood and the threat of pursuit seemed to lessen.

"Then why did you run away from our camp?"

"They were going to sacrifice me!"

"They hadn't decided that yet. That's why they were arguing."

"So what should I have done? Waited to find out?"

"The Prophecy," Renn said coldly, "could mean two

different things. If you hadn't run away, you would have learned that."

"And I suppose you're going to tell me," said Torak, "because you know everything."

She heaved a sigh. "The Prophecy could mean that we sacrifice you and give your blood to the Mountain— and by doing so, destroy the bear. That's what Hord thinks it means. He wants to kill you, so that *he* can take your blood to the Mountain." She paused. "Saeunn thinks it means something else: that only you can find the Mountain and destroy the bear."

Torak turned and stared at her. "Me. Destroy the bear."

She looked him up and down. "I know; it doesn't seem possible. But Saeunn's sure of it. So am I. The Listener must find the Mountain of the World Spirit— and then, with the Spirit's help, he must destroy the bear."

Torak blinked. It couldn't be. They'd got it wrong.

"Why must you go on denying it?" Renn said angrily. "You *are* the Listener. You know you are. You fought with air, just as the Prophecy says. You spoke with silence: that whistle. And the very first words of the Prophecy say that the Listener can talk to the other hunters in the Forest—and you *can* talk to them, because your father put you in a wolf den when you were small."

Torak narrowed his eyes. "How do you know about that?"

"Because I listened."

They followed the river west. As he walked, Torak heard the soft piping of bullfinches eating the brambles; a nuthatch tapping a branch for grubs. With all these birds around, the bear couldn't be anywhere close. . . .

Suddenly, Wolf pricked his ears and twitched his whiskers.

"Down!" hissed Torak, pulling Renn with him.

Moments later, two dugout canoes slid past. Torak had a good view of the one closest to him. The man who paddled it had short brown hair cut in bangs on the brow. He wore a stiff hide mantle across his broad shoulders, and a boar's tusk on a thong at his breast. A black slate throwing axe lay on his knees. Like his companion in the other canoe, he was scanning the banks as he sliced the water with powerful strokes. It was only too clear what he was seeking.

"Boar Clan," whispered Renn in Torak's ear. "Fin-Kedinn must have gotten them to help search for us."

Torak was instantly suspicious. "How did they know we'd come this way? Did you leave them some kind of trail?"

She rolled her eyes. "Why would I do that?"

"For all I know, you're leading me to some other clan, to be sacrificed."

"Or maybe," she said wearily, "those Boar Clan were passing this way because their autumn camp is downstream, and—" She stopped. "How did you know they were coming?"

"I didn't. Wolf told me."

She looked startled—then alarmed. "You really can talk to him, can't you?"

Torak did not reply.

She stood up, struggling to overcome her unease. "They've gone. It's time we headed north." She replaced her arrow in her quiver and slung her bow over her shoulder, and for a moment Torak thought she was having a change of heart. Then she drew her knife and jabbed at him to get moving.

They reached a streamlet tumbling out of a rocky gorge and started to climb. Torak began to feel dizzy with tiredness. He hadn't slept the night before, and hadn't eaten for over a day.

At last he couldn't go another step, and sank to his knees. Wolf jumped out of his arms, falling over his paws in his eagerness to reach the water.

"What are you doing?" cried Renn. "We can't stop here!"

"We just did," snarled Torak. He grabbed a handful of soapwort leaves, mashed them in water, and washed off the last of the wolverine dung. Then he bent and drank his fill.

Feeling better, he rummaged in his pack for one of the rolls of dried roe buck that he'd prepared—what seemed like moons ago. After biting off a piece and tossing it to Wolf, he began to eat. It tasted wonderful. Already he could feel the deer's strength coursing through him.

Renn hesitated, then unslung her pack and knelt, but still with her knife trained on Torak. Plunging one hand into her pack, she brought out three thin, reddish-brown cakes. She held one out to him.

He took it and bit off a small fragment. It tasted rich and salty, with an aromatic tang.

"Dried salmon," said Renn with her mouth full. "We pound it with deer fat and juniper berries. It stays good all winter."

To his surprise, she held out a salmon cake to Wolf.

He pointedly ignored it.

Renn hesitated, then gave the cake to Torak. He rubbed it between his palms to mask her scent with his, then offered it to Wolf, who gulped it down.

Renn tried not to show her hurt. "So?" she said with a shrug. "I know he doesn't like me."

"That's because you keep shoving him in bags," said Torak.

"Only for his own good."

"He doesn't know that."

"Can't you tell him?"

"There's no way of saying it in wolf talk." He took another bite of salmon cake. Then he asked something that had been bothering him. "Why did you bring him?"

"What?"

"Wolf. You got him out of the camp. It can't have been easy. Why?"

She paused. "You seem to need him. I don't know why. But I thought it might be important."

He was tempted to tell her that Wolf was his guide, but checked himself. He didn't trust her. She'd been useful for helping him evade the Ravens, but that didn't change the fact that she'd taken his weapons and called him a coward. And she still had her knife pointed straight at him.

The gorge got steeper. Torak judged it safe to let Wolf walk, and the cub plodded before him with drooping tail. Wolf didn't like the climb any more than Torak.

Around midafternoon, they reached a ridge over-looking a broad, wooded valley. Torak caught the far-away glitter of a river through the trees.

"That's the Widewater," said Renn. "It's the biggest river in this part of the Forest. It flows down from the ice rivers in the High Mountains and makes Lake Axehead, then goes over the Thunder Falls and on to the Sea. We camp down there in early summer for the salmon. Sometimes, if the wind's in the east, you can hear the Falls. . . ." Her voice trailed off.

Torak guessed that she was wondering how her clan would punish her for helping their captive escape. If she hadn't called him a coward, he might have felt sorry for her.

"We'll cut across the valley," she said more briskly. "It should be easy to ford the river where those meadows are. Then we can head north—"

"No," said Torak suddenly. He pointed at Wolf. The cub had found an elk trail that wound into a dense wood of tall spruce dripping with beard-moss. He was waiting for them to follow.

"That way," said Torak. "Up the valley. Not across it."

"But that's east. If we head east, we'll reach the High Mountains too soon. That'll make going north much harder."

"Which way will Fin-Kedinn go?" said Torak.

"West for a while along the trails, then north."

"Well, then. Heading east sounds like a good idea."

She frowned. "Is this some kind of trick?"

"Look," he said. "We're heading east because Wolf says we should. He knows the way."

"What? What do you mean?"

"I mean," he said quietly, "that he knows the way to the Mountain."

She stared at him. Then she snorted. "That little cub?"

Torak nodded.

"I don't believe you."

"I don't care," said Torak.

Wolf *hated* the female tailless.

He'd hated her from the first moment he'd smelled her, as she pointed the Long-Claw-That-Flies at his pack-brother. What a thing to do. As if Tall Tailless was some kind of prey!

After that, the female tailless had done terrible things. She'd wrenched Wolf away from Tall Tailless and pushed him into a strange, airless Den, where he was bumped around so much that he'd been sick.

Even worse was the way she behaved toward Tall Tailless. Didn't she know that he was the lead wolf? She was so sharp and disrespectful when she yipped at him in tailless talk. Why didn't Tall Tailless just snarl and chase her away?

Now, as Wolf trotted along the trail, he was relieved to hear that she was several strides behind. Good. She should stay away.

He paused to munch some lingonberries at the side of the trail, spat out a bad one, and moved on, feeling the dry earth beneath his pads and the warmth of the Hot Bright Eye on his back. He raised his muzzle to catch the scents wafting from the valley: some jays and a few stale elk droppings; several storm-broken spruce;

lots of willowherb and withered blueberries. All were good, interesting smells; but beneath them was the cold, terrifying scent of the Fast Wet.

Fear snapped at Wolf afresh. Somehow, he and Tall Tailless had to get across the Fast Wet. The crossing place was still many lopes ahead, but already Wolf could hear it roaring. It was so loud that soon even his poor, half-deaf pack-brother would hear it.

There was danger ahead, and Wolf longed to turn back, but he knew that he couldn't. The Pull was getting stronger: the Pull that was like the Den pull, but not.

Suddenly, Wolf caught another scent. He flared his nostrils to take it in. His ears went back. This was bad. *Bad bad bad.*

Wolf spun around and raced back toward Tall Tailless.

FOURTEEN

"What is it?" whispered Renn, staring at the terrified cub.

"I don't know," murmured Torak. His skin began to prickle. He couldn't hear any birds.

Renn took his knife from her belt and tossed it over to him.

He caught it with a nod.

"We should turn back," she said.

"We can't. This is the way to the Mountain."

Wolf's amber eyes were dark with fear. He padded slowly forward: head down, hackles raised.

Torak and Renn followed as quietly as they could.

Junipers snagged their boots. Beard-moss trailed thin fingers against their faces. The trees were utterly still, waiting to see what would happen.

"Maybe it isn't . . ." said Renn. "I mean, it could be a lynx. Or a wolverine."

Torak didn't believe that any more than she did.

They rounded a bend and came to a fallen birch that was bleeding from deep claw marks gouged in its bark.

Neither spoke. Both knew that bears sometimes claw at trees to mark their range or frighten off other hunters.

Wolf approached the birch for a better sniff. Torak followed—then gave a sigh of relief. "Badger."

"Are you sure?" said Renn.

"The scratches are smaller than a bear's, and there's mud on the bark." He circled the tree. "It got its front claws clogged with earth, digging for worms. Stopped here to scrape them clean. Went back to its sett. That way . . ." He waved a hand east.

"How do you know all that?" said Renn. "Did Wolf tell you?"

"No. The Forest did." He caught her puzzled glance. "A while back I saw a robin with some badger hairs in its beak. It came from the east." He shrugged.

"You're good at tracking, aren't you?"

"Fa was better."

"Well you're better than me," said Renn. She didn't

sound envious; she was merely acknowledging a fact. "But why would a badger have frightened Wolf?"

"I don't think it did," said Torak. "I think it was something else."

She took his axe, bow, and quiver, and held them out. "Here. You'd better take these."

They crept up the trail. Wolf went first, Torak next, scanning for signs, and Renn last, straining to see through the trees.

They'd gone another fifty paces when Torak stopped so abruptly that she walked into him.

The young beech tree was still moaning, but it hadn't long to live. The bear had reared on its hind legs to vent its fury: snapping off the entire top of the tree, ripping away the bark in long bleeding tatters, and slashing deep gouges high on the trunk. Terrifyingly high. If Renn had stood on Torak's shoulders, she wouldn't have been able to reach the lowest claw mark.

"No bear could be that enormous," she whispered.

Torak did not reply. He was back in the blue autumn dusk, helping Fa to pitch camp. Torak had made a joke, and Fa was laughing. Then the Forest exploded. Ravens screamed. Pines cracked. And out of the dark beneath the trees surged a deeper darkness. . . .

"It's old," said Renn.

"What?" said Torak.

She gestured at the trunk. "The tree-blood has

hardened. Look, it's almost black."

He studied the tree. She was right. The bear had clawed the bark at least two days before.

But he couldn't share Renn's relief. She didn't know the worst of it.

With each kill, Fa had said, *its power will grow. . . . When the red eye is highest . . . the bear will be invincible.*

Here was the proof. On the night when the bear had attacked, it had been huge. But not this huge.

"It's getting bigger," he said.

"What?" said Renn.

Torak told her what Fa had said.

"But—that's not even a moon away."

"I know."

A few paces off the trail, he found three long black hairs snagged on a twig at about head height. He stepped back sharply. "It went that way." He pointed down into the valley. "See how the branches have sprung back in a slightly different pattern."

But that didn't reassure him. The bear could have returned by another trail.

Then, from deep in the undergrowth, came the sharp *tak tak* of a wren.

Torak breathed out. "I don't think it's anywhere close. Otherwise that wren wouldn't be calling."

As night fell, they made a shelter of bent hazel saplings and leaf mold by a muddy stream. Holly trees gave a pretense of cover, and they lit a small fire and ate a few slips of dried meat. They didn't dare risk the salmon cakes; the bear would have smelled them from many daywalks away.

It was a cold night, and Torak sat hunched in his sleeping-sack, listening to the faint, faraway roar that Renn said was the Thunder Falls.

Why had Fa never told him about the Prophecy? Why was he the Listener? What did it mean?

Beside him, Wolf slept with ears twitching. Renn sat watching a beetle clamber down from the firewood.

Torak now knew that he could trust her. She'd risked a lot to help him, and he couldn't have escaped without her. It was a new feeling, having someone on his side. He said, "I need to tell you something."

Renn reached for a twig and helped the beetle off a branch.

"Before he died," said Torak, "my father made me swear an oath. To find the Mountain, or die trying." He paused. "I don't know why he made me swear. But I did. And I'll do my best."

She nodded, and he saw that for the first time she truly believed him. "There's something I've got to tell you, too," she said. "It's about the Prophecy." Frowning, she turned the twig in her fingers. "When—

if—you find the Mountain, you can't just ask the Spirit
for help. You've got to prove that you're worthy. Saeunn
told me last night. She said that when the crippled
wanderer made the bear, he broke the pact, because he
made a creature that kills without purpose. He angered
the World Spirit. It'll take a great deal to get it to help."

Torak tried to swallow. "What will it take?"

She met his eyes. "You've got to bring it the three
strongest pieces of the Nanuak."

Torak looked at her blankly.

"Saeunn says that the Nanuak is like a great river
that never ends. Every living thing has a part of it
inside it. Hunters, prey, rocks, trees. Sometimes a
special part of it forms, like foam on the river. When it
does, it's incredibly powerful." She hesitated. "That's
what you've got to find. If you don't, the World Spirit
won't help you. And then you'll never destroy the
bear."

Torak caught his breath. "Three pieces of the
Nanuak," he said hoarsely. "What are they? How do I
find them?"

"Nobody knows. All we have is a riddle." She shut
her eyes and recited,

> *"Deepest of all, the drowned sight.*
> *Oldest of all, the stone bite.*
> *Coldest of all, the darkest light."*

A breeze sprang up. The holly trees gave a prickly murmur.

"What does it mean?" asked Torak.

Renn opened her eyes. "Nobody knows."

He bowed his head to his knees. "So I've got to find a mountain that nobody's ever seen. And work out the answer to a riddle that nobody's ever solved. And kill a bear that nobody can fight."

Renn sucked in her breath. "You've got to try."

Torak was silent. Then he said, "Why did Saeunn tell you all this? Why you?"

Renn shrugged. "She just did. She thinks I should be a Mage when I'm grown."

"Don't you want to be?"

"No! But I suppose—maybe there's a purpose in these things. If she hadn't told me, I wouldn't have been able to tell you."

Another silence. Then Renn wriggled out of her sleeping-sack. "I'll take our packs outside. We don't want the food smell to draw the bear to the shelter."

When she'd gone, Torak curled up on his side and lost himself in the fiery heart of the embers. Around him, the Forest creaked in its sleep, dreaming its deep green dreams. He thought of the thousands and thousands of tree-spirits thronging the darkness: waiting for him, and him alone, to deliver them from the bear.

He thought of the golden birch and the scarlet

rowan, and the brilliant green oaks. He thought of the teeming prey; of the lakes and rivers full of fish; of all the different kinds of wood and bark and stone that were there for the taking if you knew where to look. The Forest had everything you could ever want. Until now he'd never realized how much he loved it.

If the bear could not be destroyed, all this would be lost.

Wolf leaped up and went off on one of his nightly hunts. Renn returned, got into her sleeping-sack without a word, and fell asleep. Torak went on staring into the fire.

There's a purpose in these things, Renn had said. In a strange way, that gave him strength. He *was* the Listener. He had sworn to find the Mountain. The Forest needed him.

He slept fitfully. He dreamed that Fa was alive again; but instead of a face, he had a blank white stone. *I am not Fa. I am the Wolf Mage. . . .*

Torak woke with a start.

He felt Wolf's breath on his face; then the downy brush of the cub's whiskers on his eyelids, and the needle-fine grooming-nibbles on his cheeks and throat.

He licked the cub's muzzle, and Wolf nuzzled his chin, then settled against him with a "humph."

"We should have crossed lower down," said Renn as they craned their necks at the Thunder Falls.

Torak wiped the spray from his face and wondered how anything in the Forest could be this angry.

All day they'd been following the calm green Widewater upstream. But now, as it thundered over a sheer wall of rock, it was appalling in its fury. Before it, the whole Forest seemed to stand and stare.

"We should have crossed lower down," Renn said again.

"We would've been seen," said Torak. "Those meadows were too exposed. Besides, Wolf wanted to stay on this side."

Renn pursed her lips. "If he's the guide, then where is he?"

"He hates fast water. His pack was drowned in a flood. But he'll be back when we've found a way to get above the falls."

"Mm," said Renn, unconvinced. Like Torak, she'd slept badly, and she'd been moody all morning. Neither of them had mentioned the riddle.

Eventually, they found a deer track that wound up the side of the falls. It was steep and muddy, and by the time they reached the top, they were exhausted and soaked in spray. Wolf was waiting for them: sitting beneath a birch tree a safe distance from the Widewater, shaking with fear.

"Where to now?" panted Renn.

Torak was watching Wolf. "We follow the river

till he tells us to cross."

"Can you swim?" asked Renn.

He nodded. "Can you?"

"Yes. Can Wolf?"

"I don't think so."

They started upstream, pushing through brambles and tangled rowan and birch. It was a cold, overcast day, and the wind scattered birch leaves onto the river like small amber arrowheads. Wolf trotted with his ears flat back. The river ran fast and smooth on its way to the falls.

They hadn't gone far when Wolf began to run up and down the bank, mewing. Torak could feel his fear. He turned to Renn. "He wants to cross, but he's frightened."

"The brambles are too thick here," said Renn. "What about farther up by those rocks?"

The rocks were smooth and splashed with treacherous-looking moss, but they reared a good half forearm out of the water. They might provide a way across.

Torak nodded.

"I'll go first," said Renn, pulling off her boots and tying them to her pack, then rolling up her leggings. She found a stick for balance and slung her pack over one shoulder, so that it wouldn't drag her down if she fell in. Her quiver and bow she carried in the other hand, high above her head.

She looked scared as she approached the water. But she made it across without faltering—until the final rock, when she had to leap for the bank, and ended up grabbing a willow branch to haul herself up.

Torak left his pack and weapons on the bank, and pulled off his boots. He would carry Wolf across, then return for his things. "Come on, Wolf," he said encouragingly. Then he said it in wolf talk, hunkering down on his haunches and making low, reassuring mewing noises.

Wolf shot under a juniper bush and refused to come out.

"Put him in your pack!" shouted Renn from the other side. "It's the only way you'll get him across!"

"If I did that," yelled Torak, "he'd never trust me again!"

He sat down in the moss on the edge of the bank. Then he yawned and stretched, to show Wolf how relaxed he was.

After a while, Wolf emerged from the juniper and came to sit beside him.

Again Torak yawned.

Wolf glanced at him, then gave a huge yawn that ended in a whine.

Slowly, Torak got to his feet and picked Wolf up in his arms, murmuring softly in wolf talk.

The rocks felt ice-cold and slippery under Torak's

bare feet. In his arms, Wolf started shivering with terror.

On the far bank, Renn held on to a birch sapling with one hand and leaned toward them. "That's it," she shouted above the thunder of the falls. "You're nearly there!"

Wolf's claws dug into Torak's jerkin.

"Last rock!" shouted Renn. "I'll grab him. . . ."

A wave slapped into the rock, splashing them with freezing water. Wolf's courage broke. Twisting frantically out of Torak's grip, he leaped for the bank, landing with his hind legs in the water and his forepaws clawing at the bank.

Renn leaned down and caught him by the scruff. "I've got him!" she yelled.

Torak lost his balance and crashed into the river.

FIFTEEN

Torak came up spluttering with cold, fighting the
river.

He was a strong swimmer, so he wasn't too worried.
He'd grab that branch jutting from the bank. . . .

The next one, then.

Behind him, he heard Renn shouting his name as
she tore through the brambles, and Wolf's urgent barks.
It occurred to him that the brambles must be very
thick, as Renn and Wolf were dropping farther and
farther behind.

The river punched him in the back, smashing him
limp as a wet leaf against a rock. He went under.

He kicked his way to the surface and was shocked to see how far he'd been carried. He couldn't hear Renn or Wolf anymore, and the waterfall was sliding closer with astonishing speed, drowning all voices but its own.

His jerkin and leggings were dragging him down. The cold had deadened his limbs to sticks of bone and flesh, working without feeling to keep his head above the surface. He couldn't see anything except white-foam waves and a blur of willows. Then even that disappeared as he went under again.

It came to him quite clearly that he would be swept over the waterfall and killed.

No time for fear. Just a distant anger that it should end like this. Poor Wolf. Who's going to look after him now? And poor Renn. Let's hope she doesn't find the body; it'll be a mess.

Death boomed at him. A rainbow flashed through the spume and spray . . . then the waves smoothed out like a skin and suddenly there was no more river in front, and it was hard to breathe as he went over. Death reached up and pulled him down, and it was shining and smooth, like the moment of falling asleep. . . .

Over and over he fell, water filling his mouth, his nose, his ears. The river swallowed him whole: He was inside it, and it roared through him, this pounding power of water. Somehow he surfaced, gulping air.

Then it pulled him down again into its swirling green depths.

The roar of the river faded. Lights flashed in his head. He sank. The water turned from blue to dark green to black. He was languid and frozen past feeling. He longed to give up and sleep.

He became aware of a faint, bubbling laughter. Hair like green waterweed trailed across his throat. Cruel faces leered at him with merciless white eyes.

Come to us! called the Hidden People of the river. *Let your souls float free of that dull, heavy flesh!*

He felt sick, as if his guts were being pulled loose.

See, see! laughed the Hidden People. *How swiftly his souls begin to drift free! How eagerly they come to us!*

Torak turned over and over like a dead fish. The Hidden People were right. It would be so easy to leave his body and let them roll him forever in their cold embrace. . . .

Wolf's desperate yowl cut through to him.

Torak opened his eyes. Silver bubbles streamed through the dark as the Hidden People fled.

Again Wolf called to him.

Wolf needed him. There was something they had to do together.

Flailing his numb stick-limbs, he began to fight his way back toward the surface. The green grew brighter. The light drew him. . . .

He'd nearly reached it when something made him look down—and he saw them. Far below, two blind white eyes staring up at him.

What were they? River pearls? The eyes of one of the Hidden People?

The Prophecy. The riddle. *Deepest of all, the drowned sight.*

His chest was bursting. If he didn't get air soon, he would die. But if he didn't swim down now and grasp those eyes—whatever they were—he would lose them forever.

He doubled over and kicked with all his might, pushing himself down.

The cold made his eyes ache, but he didn't dare shut them. Closer and closer he swam. . . . He reached out toward the bottom—he grasped a handful of icy mud. He had them! No way to make sure—the mud was swirling thick around him, and he couldn't risk opening his fist in case they slipped free—but he could feel the weight of them dragging him down. He twisted around and kicked back toward the light.

But his strength was failing, and he rose with agonizing slowness, hampered by his sodden clothes. More lights flashed in his head. More watery laughter. *Too late*, whispered the Hidden People. *You'll never reach the light now! Stay here with us, boy with the drifting souls. Stay here forever. . . .*

Something grabbed his leg and pulled him down.

He kicked. Couldn't get free. Something was gripping his legging just above the ankle. He twisted around to wrench himself free, but the grip held tight. He tried to draw his knife from its sheath, but he'd tightened the strap around the hilt before starting the crossing, and he couldn't get it loose.

Anger boiled up inside him. Get away from me! he shouted inside his head. You can't have me—and you can't have the Nanuak!

Fury lent him strength and he kicked out savagely. The grip on his leg broke. Something gave a gurgling howl and sank into darkness. Torak shot upward.

He exploded from the water, gulping great chestfuls of air. Through the glare of the sun he glimpsed a sheet of green river, and an overhanging branch approaching him fast. With his free hand he reached for it—and missed. Pain exploded in his head.

He knew that he hadn't been knocked out. He could still feel the slap of the river, and hear his breath—but his eyes were open and staring, and he couldn't see.

Panic seized him. Not blind, he thought. No, no *please*, not blind.

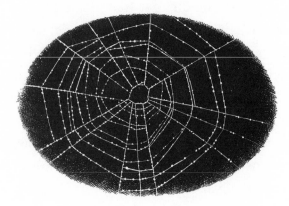

SIXTEEN

The female tailless was whimpering and waving her forepaws, so Wolf left her and hurtled down the track.

When he smelled Tall Tailless among the willows, he began to whimper too. His pack-brother was slumped over a log, half in the Wet. He smelled strongly of blood and wasn't moving at all.

Wolf licked his cold cheek, but Tall Tailless didn't stir. Was he Not-Breath? Wolf put up his muzzle and howled.

A clumsy crashing announced the female tailless. Wolf leaped to defend his pack-brother, but she pushed him away, hooked her forepaws under Tall Tailless's shoulders, and hauled him out of the Wet.

Despite himself, Wolf was impressed.

He watched as she put her forepaws on Tall Tailless's chest and pressed down hard. Tall Tailless began to cough! Tall Tailless had breath again!

But just as Wolf was jumping onto his pack-brother to snuffle-lick his muzzle, he was batted away! Heedless of Wolf's warning growls, the female pulled Tall Tailless to his legs and they staggered up the bank. Tall Tailless kept blundering into hazel bushes, as if he couldn't see.

Watchfully, Wolf walked beside them, relaxing a little when they reached a Den a good distance from the Fast Wet: a proper Den, not a small, airless one.

Still the female wouldn't let Wolf near his pack-brother. Snarling, Wolf slammed her with his body. Instead of moving away, she picked up a stick and threw it out of the Den, pointing at it and then at Wolf.

Wolf ignored her and turned back to Tall Tailless, who was trying to tug off his pelt. Finally, Tall Tailless had only the long dark fur on his head. He lay curled on his side with his eyes shut, shaking with cold. His poor furless underpelt was no use at all.

Wolf leaned against him to warm him up, while the female tailless quickly brought to life the Bright Beast-That-Bites-Hot. Tall Tailless moved closer to the warmth, and Wolf watched anxiously in case he got his paws bitten.

That was when Wolf noticed that one of Tall Tailless's forepaws held something that was giving off a strange glow.

Wolf sniffed at it—and backed away. It smelled of hunter and prey and Fast Wet and tree, all chewed up together; and from it came a high, thin humming, so high that Wolf could only just catch it.

Wolf was frightened. He knew that he was in the presence of something very, very powerful.

Torak huddled in his sleeping-sack, shivering un-controllably. His head was on fire and his whole body felt like one big bruise, but worst of all, he couldn't see. *Blind, blind*, thudded his heart.

Above the crackle of the fire he heard Renn muttering angrily. "Were you *trying* to get yourself killed?"

"What?" he said, but it came out as a mumble, because his mouth was thick with the salty sweetness of blood.

"You'd nearly reached the surface," said Renn, pressing what felt like cobwebs to his forehead, "then you turned around and swam, deliberately swam, back down again!"

He realized that she didn't know about the Nanuak.

But his fist was so cold that he couldn't unclench it to show her.

He felt Wolf's hot tongue on his face. A chink of light appeared. Then a big black nose. Torak's spirits soared. "I cad thee!" he said.

"What?" snapped Renn. "Well of course you can see! You cut your forehead when you hit that branch, and the blood got in your eyes. Scalp wounds bleed a lot. Didn't you know that?"

Torak was so relieved that he would have laughed if his teeth hadn't been chattering so violently.

He saw that they were in a small cave with earth walls. A birchwood fire was burning fiercely, and already his sodden clothes, hanging from tree roots jutting through the ceiling, were beginning to steam. The thunder of the falls was loud, and from its sound, and the view of treetops at the cave mouth, he guessed they must be some way up the side of the valley. He couldn't remember getting there. Renn must have dragged him. He wondered how she'd managed it.

She was kneeling beside him, looking shaken. "You've been very, very lucky," she said. "Now hold still." From her medicine pouch she took some dried yarrow leaves and crumbled them in her palm. Then, having picked off the cobwebs, she pressed the yarrow leaves to his forehead. They stuck tight to the wound in an instant scab.

Torak shut his eyes and listened to the never-ending fury of the falls. Wolf crawled into the sleeping-sack with him, wriggling till he got comfortable. Torak felt gloriously furry and warm as the cub licked his shoulder. Torak licked his muzzle in reply.

When he awoke, he wasn't shivering anymore, and he was still clutching the Nanuak. He could feel its weight in his fist.

Wolf was nosing about in the back of the cave, and Renn was sorting herbs in her lap. Torak's pack, boots, quiver, and bow were neatly piled behind her. He realized that to retrieve them she must have crossed the river again. Twice.

"Renn," he said.

"What," she said without looking up. From her tone, he could tell that she was still cross.

"You got me out of the river. You got me all the way up here. You even fetched my things. I can't imagine . . . I mean, that was brave."

She did not reply.

"Renn," he said again.

"*What.*"

"I had to swim down. I had to."

"Why?"

Awkwardly, he brought out the hand that held the Nanuak and unclenched his fingers.

As soon as he did, the fire seemed to sink. Shadows

leaped on the cave walls. The air seemed to crackle, like the moment after a lightning strike.

Wolf stopped nosing and gave a warning grunt. Renn went very still.

The river eyes lay in Torak's palm in a nest of green mud, glowing faintly, like the moon on a misty night.

As he gazed at them, Torak felt an echo of the sickness that had tugged at him at the bottom of the river. "This is it, isn't it?" he said. "'*Deepest of all, the drowned sight.*' The first part of the Nanuak."

The color had drained from Renn's face. "Don't—move," she said, and scrambled out of the cave, returning soon after with a bunch of scarlet rowan leaves.

"Lucky there's mud on your hand," she said. "You mustn't let it touch your skin. It might suck out your own part of the world-soul."

"Is that what was happening?" he murmured. "In the river I was beginning to feel—dizzy." He told her about the Hidden People.

She looked horrified. "If they'd caught you . . ." She made the sign of the hand to ward off evil. "I can't believe you've just been sleeping with those in your fist. There's no time to lose."

Bringing out a little black pouch from inside her jerkin, she stuffed it with the rowan leaves. "The leaves should protect us," she said, "and the pouch should help too; it's raven skin." Grasping Torak's wrist, she tipped the river eyes into the pouch and drew the neck tight.

As soon as the Nanuak was hidden, the flames grew, and the shadows shrank. The air in the cave stopped crackling.

Torak felt as if a weight had been taken from him. He watched Wolf pad over and lie down beside Renn with his muzzle between his paws, gazing at the pouch on her lap and whining softly.

"D'you think he can smell it?" she asked.

"Or maybe hear it," said Torak. "I don't know."

Renn shivered. "Just as long as nothing else can, too."

SEVENTEEN

Torak woke at dawn feeling stiff and sore. But he could move all four limbs, and nothing felt broken, so he decided he was better.

Renn was kneeling at the mouth of the cave, trying to feed Wolf a handful of crowberries. She was frowning with concentration as she held out her hand. Wolf edged cautiously forward—then jerked back again. At last he decided he could trust her, and snuffled up the berries. Renn laughed as his whiskers tickled her palm.

She caught Torak looking and stopped laughing, embarrassed to be seen making friends with the cub. "How do you feel?" she asked.

"Better."

"You don't look it. You'll need to rest for at least a day." She got to her feet. "I'm going hunting. We should keep the dried food for when we need it."

Torak sat up painfully. "I'm coming too."

"No you're not. You should rest—"

"But my clothes are dry, and I need to move around." He didn't tell her the real reason, which was that he hated caves. He and Fa used to shelter in them sometimes, but Torak always ended up outside. It felt all wrong to be sleeping between solid walls, cut off from the wind and the Forest. It felt like being swallowed.

Renn sighed. "Promise that as soon as we make a kill, you'll come back here and rest."

Torak promised.

Getting dressed hurt more than he'd expected, and by the time he'd finished, his eyes were watering. To his relief, Renn didn't notice, as she was preparing for the hunt. She combed her hair with an ashwood comb carved like a raven's claw, then tied it back in a horse-tail and stuck in an owl feather for hunting luck. Next, she smeared ash on her skin to mask her scent, and oiled her bow with a couple of crushed hazelnuts, chanting: "May the clan guardian fly with me and make the hunt successful."

Torak was surprised. "We prepare for hunting in the

same way. Except we say, 'May the clan guardian *run* with me.' And we don't oil our bows every time."

"That's just something I do," said Renn. Lovingly she held it up so that the oiled wood gleamed. "Fin-Kedinn made it for me when I was seven, just after Fa was killed. It's yewwood, seasoned for four summers. Sapwood on its back for stretch, heartwood on its belly for strength. He made the quiver, too. Wove the wicker himself, and let me choose the decoration. A zigzag band of red and white willow."

She paused, and her face became shadowed as she remembered. "I never knew my mother; Fa was everything. When he was killed, I was crying so hard. Then Fin-Kedinn came, and I hit him with my fists. He didn't move. Just stood there like an oak tree, letting me hit him. Then he said, 'He was my brother. I will look after you.' And I knew that he would." She scowled, sucking in her lips.

Torak knew that she was missing her uncle, and probably worrying about him too, as he tracked her through the bear-haunted Forest. To give her time, he made his own preparations and gathered his weapons. Then he said, "Come on. Let's go hunting."

She nodded once, then shouldered her quiver.

It was a bright, cold morning, and the Forest had never looked so beautiful. Scarlet rowan trees and golden birch blazed like flames against the dark-green spruce. Blueberry bushes glittered with thousands of tiny, frost-spangled spiders' webs. Frozen moss crunched underfoot. A pair of inquisitive magpies followed them from tree to tree, bickering. The bear must be far away.

Unfortunately, Torak didn't get long to enjoy it. Around midmorning, Wolf startled a clutch of willow grouse, who shot skyward with indignant gobbles. The birds flew fast and into the sun, so Torak didn't even bother taking aim, knowing he'd never hit one. To his astonishment, Renn nocked an arrow and let fly, and a willow grouse thudded into the moss.

Torak's jaw dropped. "How did you manage that?"

Renn reddened. "Well. I practice a lot."

"But—I've never seen shooting that good. Are you the best in your clan?"

She looked uncomfortable.

"Is there anyone better?

"Um. Not really." Still embarrassed, she waded off through the blueberry bushes to retrieve the grouse. "Here." She flashed him her sharp-toothed grin. "Remember your promise? Now you've got to go back and rest."

Torak took the grouse. If he'd known she was such a good shot, he'd never have promised.

When Renn returned to the cave, they had a feast. From the hooting of a young owl, they knew that the bear was far away; and Renn judged that they'd come far enough east to have escaped the Ravens. Besides, they needed hot food.

Renn wrapped two small pieces of grouse in dock leaves and left them for the clan guardians, while Torak moved the fire to the mouth of the cave, as he was determined not to spend another night inside. Half filling Renn's cooking skin with water, he hung it by the fire; then, using a split branch, he dropped in red-hot stones to heat it up and added the plucked and jointed willow grouse. Soon he was stirring a fragrant stew flavored with crow garlic and big, fleshy wood mushrooms.

They ate most of the meat, leaving a little for daymeal, and sopped up the juices with hawkbit roots baked in the embers. After that came a wonderful mash that Renn made of late lingonberries and hazelnuts, and finally some beechnuts, which they burst by the fire and peeled to get at the small, rich nuts inside.

By the time he'd finished, Torak felt as if he need never eat again. He settled down by the fire to mend the rip in his leggings where the Hidden People had grabbed him. Renn sat some way off, trimming the flights on her arrows, and Wolf lay between them licking his paws clean, having swiftly despatched the joint of grouse that Torak had saved for him.

For a while there was a companionable silence, and

Torak felt contented, even hopeful. After all, he'd found the first piece of the Nanuak. That must count for something.

Suddenly, Wolf leaped to his feet and raced out of the firelight. Moments later he returned, circling the fire and making agitated little grunt-whines.

"What is it?" whispered Renn.

Torak was on his feet, watching Wolf. He shook his head. "I can't make it out. 'Kill smell. Old kill. Move.' Something like that."

They stared into the darkness.

"We shouldn't have lit a fire," said Renn.

"Too late now," said Torak.

Wolf stopped the grunt-whines and raised his muzzle, gazing skyward.

Torak looked up—and the remains of his good humor vanished. To the east, above the distant blackness of the High Mountains, the red eye of the Great Auroch glared down at them. It was impossible to miss: a vicious crimson, throbbing with malice. Torak couldn't take his eyes from it. He could feel its power: sending strength to the bear, sapping his own will of hope and resolve.

"What chance do we have against the bear?" he said. "I mean, really, what chance do we have?"

"I don't know," said Renn.

"How are we going to find the other two pieces of

the Nanuak? *'Oldest of all, the stone bite. Coldest of all, the darkest light.'* What does that even mean?"

Renn did not reply.

At last he dragged his gaze from the sky and sat down by the fire. The red eye seemed to glare at him from the embers.

Behind him, Renn stirred. "Look, Torak, it's the First Tree!"

He raised his head.

The eye had been blotted out. Instead, a silent, ever-changing green glow filled the sky. Now a vast swathe of light twisted in a voiceless wind; then the swathe vanished, and shimmering pale-green waves rippled across the stars. The First Tree stretched for-ever, shining its miraculous fire upon the Forest.

As Torak gazed at it, a spark of hope rekindled. He'd always loved watching the First Tree on frosty nights, while Fa told the story of the Beginning. The First Tree meant good luck in hunting; maybe it would bring luck to him, too.

"I think it's a good sign," said Renn as if she'd heard his thoughts. "I've been wondering. Was it really luck that you found the Nanuak? I mean, why did you fall into the very part of the river where it lay? I don't think that was by chance. I think—you were meant to find it."

He threw her a questioning glance.

"Maybe," she said slowly, "the Nanuak was *put* in

your way, but then it was up to you to decide what to do about it. When you saw it at the bottom of the river, you *could* have decided it was too dangerous to try for. But you didn't. You risked your life to get it. Maybe— that was part of the test."

It was a good thought, and it made Torak feel a little better. He fell asleep watching the silent green boughs of the First Tree, while Wolf sped out of the cave on some mysterious errand of his own.

Wolf left the Den and loped up to the ridge above the valley to catch the smell on the wind: a powerful smell of rotten prey like a very old kill—except that it moved.

As he ran, Wolf felt with joy how his pads were toughening, his limbs getting stronger with every Dark that passed. He loved to run, and he wished that Tall Tailless did, too. But at times his pack-brother could be terribly slow.

As Wolf neared the ridge, he heard the roar of the Thundering Wet, and the sound of a hare feeding in the next valley. Overhead, he saw the Bright White Eye with her many little cubs. It was all as it should be. Except for that smell.

At the top of the ridge he lifted his muzzle to catch the scent-laden winds and again he caught it: quite close, and coming closer. Racing back into the valley, he soon found it: the strange, shuffling thing that smelled so rotten.

He got near enough to observe it clearly in the dark, although he was careful not to let it know that he was near. To his surprise he found that it was not an old kill after all. It had breath and claws, and it moved in an odd shambling walk, growling to itself while spit trailed from its muzzle.

What puzzled Wolf most was that he couldn't catch what it was feeling. Its mind seemed broken; scattered like old bones. Wolf had never sensed such a thing before.

He watched it make its way up the slope toward the Den where the taillesses were sleeping. It prowled closer. . . .

Just as Wolf was about to attack, it shook itself and shambled away. But through the tangle of its broken thoughts, Wolf sensed that it would be back.

EIGHTEEN

The fog stole up on them like a thief in the night.
When Torak crawled stiffly from his sleeping-sack, the valley below had disappeared. The Breath of the World Spirit had swallowed it whole.

He yawned. Wolf had woken him often in the night, racing about and uttering urgent half barks: *kill smell— watch*. It didn't make sense. Every time Torak went to look, there was nothing but a stink of carrion and an uneasy feeling of being watched.

"Maybe he just hates fog," said Renn grumpily as she rolled up her sleeping-sack. "I know I do. In fog, nothing's what it seems."

"I don't think it's that," said Torak, watching Wolf snuffing the air.

"Well, what is it, then?"

"I don't know. It's as if something's out there. Not the bear. Not the Ravens. Something else."

"What do you mean?"

"I told you, I don't know. But we should be on our guard." Thoughtfully, he put more wood on the fire to heat up the rest of the stew for daymeal.

With an anxious frown, Renn counted their arrows. "Fourteen between us. Not nearly enough. Do you know how to knap flint?"

Torak shook his head. "My hands aren't strong enough. Fa was going to teach me next summer. What about you?"

"The same. We'll have to be careful. There's no telling how far it is to the Mountain. And we'll need more meat."

"Maybe we'll catch something today."

"In this fog?"

She was right. The fog was so thick that they couldn't see Wolf five paces ahead. It was the kind that the clans call the smoke-frost: an icy breath that descends from the High Mountains at the start of winter, blackening berries and sending small creatures scuttling for their burrows.

Wolf led them along an auroch trail that wound

north up the side of the valley: a chilly climb through frost-brittle bracken. The fog muffled sounds and made distances hard to judge. Trees loomed with alarming suddenness. Once, they shot a reindeer, only to find that they'd hit a log. That meant a frustrating struggle to dig out the arrowheads, which they couldn't afford to lose. Twice, Torak thought he saw a figure in the undergrowth, but when he ran to look, he found nothing.

It took all morning to climb the ridge, and all afternoon to scramble down into the next valley, where a silent pine forest guarded a slumbering river.

"Do you realize," said Renn as they huddled in a hasty shelter after a cheerless nightmeal, "that we haven't seen a single reindeer? They should be everywhere by now."

"I've been thinking that too," said Torak. Like Renn, he knew that the snow on the fells should be driving the herds into the Forest, to grow fat on moss and mushrooms. Sometimes they ate so many mushrooms that they even tasted of them.

"What will the clans do if the reindeer don't come?" said Renn.

Torak didn't answer. Reindeer meant survival: meat, bedding, and clothes.

He wondered what he was going to do for winter clothes. Renn had had the foresight to put hers on before she'd left the Raven camp, but she hadn't been able to steal any for him, so all he had was his summer buckskin: not nearly as warm as the furry parka and leggings that he and Fa made every autumn.

Even if they did find prey, there'd be no time to make clothes. Beyond the fog, the red eye of the Great Auroch was climbing ever higher.

Torak shut his eyes to push the thought away, and eventually fell into an uneasy sleep. But whenever he awoke in the night, he caught that strange carrion stink.

Next morning dawned colder and foggier than ever, and even Wolf seemed dejected as he led them upstream. They reached a fallen oak bridging the river and crawled over it on their hands and knees. Soon afterward, the trail forked. To the left, it wound into a valley of misty beech trees; to the right, it disappeared up a dank gully, its steep sides an uninviting jumble of moss-covered boulders.

To their dismay, Wolf took the right-hand trail.

"That can't be right!" cried Renn. "The Mountain's in the north! Why is he forever going east?"

Torak shook his head. "It feels wrong to me, too. But he seems sure."

Renn snorted. She was clearly having doubts again.

Looking at Wolf waiting patiently, Torak felt a twinge of guilt. The cub wasn't even four moons old. At this age, he should be playing by his den, not traipsing over hills. "I think," he said, "we ought to trust him."

"Mm," murmured Renn.

Hoisting their packs higher on their aching shoulders, they entered the gully.

They hadn't gone ten paces before they knew that it didn't want them. Towering spruce trees warned them back with arms spread wide. A boulder crashed in front of them; another struck the path just behind Renn. The stink of carrion grew stronger. But if it came from a kill site, it was a strange one, for they heard no ravens.

The fog closed in until they could barely see two paces ahead. All they could hear was the drip, drip of mist on the bracken, and the gurgle of a stream rushing between fern-choked banks. Torak began to see bear shapes in the fog. He watched Wolf for the least sign of alarm, but the cub plodded along, unafraid.

At midday—or what felt like midday—they halted for a rest. Wolf slumped down, panting, and Renn shrugged off her pack. Her face was pinched, her hair soaking. "I saw some reeds back there. I'm going to plait myself a hood." Hanging their quivers and bows on a branch, she moved off through the ferns. Wolf heaved himself up and padded after her.

Torak squatted at the edge of the stream to refill the waterskins. It wasn't long before he heard Renn coming back. "That was quick," he said.

"*Out!*" bellowed a voice behind him. "Out of the Walker's Valley or the Walker slits throats!"

Torak spun round and found himself staring up at an unbelievably filthy man towering over him with a knife.

In an instant he took in a ruined face as rough as tree bark; waist-length hair matted with filth; a rancid cape of slimy yellow reeds. And at last the carrion stink was explained, for around the man's neck hung a pigeon's softly rotting carcass.

In fact, everything about the man seemed to be rotting: from his empty, festering eye socket to his toothless black gums and his shattered nose, from which hung a loop of greenish-yellow slime. "*Out!*" he bellowed, waving a green slate knife. "Narik and the Walker say out!"

Quickly, Torak put both fists over his heart in the sign of friendship. "Please—we come as friends. We mean you no harm—"

"But they already *did* harm!" roared the man. "They bring it with them to the beautiful valley! All night the Walker watches! All night he waits to see if they will bring harm to his valley!"

"What harm?" Torak said desperately. "We didn't mean it!"

There was a stirring in the bracken and Wolf threw

himself at Torak. Torak clutched the cub close and felt the small heart hammering.

The man didn't notice. He'd heard Renn creeping up behind him. "Sneaking up, is she?" he snarled, lurching round and waving his knife in her face.

Renn dodged backward, but that only made him angrier.

"Does she want them in the water?" he cried, snatching their bows and quivers from the branch and holding them out over the stream. "Does she want to see them swim, the pretty arrows and the shiny, shiny bows?"

Mute with horror, Renn shook her head.

"Then they drop knives and axes quick, or in they go!"

They both knew that they didn't have a choice, so they tossed their remaining weapons at his feet, and he stowed them swiftly under his cape.

"What do you want us to do?" asked Torak, his heart hammering as fast as Wolf's.

"Get *out*!" roared the man. "The Walker *told* them! *Narik* told them! And the anger of Narik is terrible!"

Both Renn and Torak looked round for Narik, whoever he was, but saw only wet trees and fog.

"We are getting out," said Renn, eyeing her bow in the enormous fist.

"Not *up* the Valley! Out!" He gestured to the side of the gully.

"But—we can't go up there," said Renn. "It's too steep—"

"No more tricks!" bellowed the Walker, and hurled her quiver into the stream.

She screamed and leaped after it, but Torak grabbed her arm. "It's too late," he told her. "It's gone." The stream was deeper and faster than it looked. Her beloved quiver had disappeared.

Renn turned on the Walker. "We were doing what you said! You didn't have to do that!"

"Oh yes he did," said the Walker with a toothless black grin. "Now they know he means it!"

"Come on, Renn," said Torak. "Let's do as he says."

Furious, Renn picked up her pack.

If their journey had been hard before, this was worse. The Walker strode behind them, forcing them almost at a run up a rocky elk trail that at times had them climbing on their hands and knees. Renn went in front, stony faced, grieving for her quiver. Wolf soon began to lag behind.

Torak turned to help him, but the Walker sliced the air a finger's breadth from his face. "On!" he shouted.

"I just want to carry—"

"On!"

Renn cut in. "You're Otter Clan, aren't you? I recognize your tattoos."

The Walker glared at her.

Torak seized his chance and hoisted the flagging cub in his arms.

"*Was* Otter Clan," muttered the Walker, clawing his neck, where the crusted skin was tattooed with wavy blue-green lines.

"Why did you leave them?" asked Renn, who was making a supreme effort to forget about her quiver and befriend him, in order to keep them alive.

"Didn't *leave*," said the Walker. "Otters leave *him*." Twisting a wing off the pigeon, he sucked it between his toothless gums, taking in with it a generous loop of slime.

Torak swayed. Renn turned pale green.

"The Walker was making spearheads," he said through a rancid mouthful, "and the flint flies at him and bites him in the head." He gave a bark of laughter, spraying them both. "Bits of him going bad, getting sewn up, going bad again. In the end his eye pops right out, and a raven eats it. Ha! Ravens like eyes."

Then his face crumpled, and he pounded his head with his fist. "Ach, but the hurts, the hurts! All the voices howling, the souls fighting in his head! That's why the Otters chase him away!"

Renn swallowed. "One of my clan lost an eye the same way," she said. "My clan is friendly with the Otters. We—we mean you no harm."

"Maybe," said the Walker, removing a bone from

his mouth and stowing it carefully inside his cape. "But they still bring it with them." All of a sudden, he halted and scanned the slopes. "But the Walker was forgetting. Narik asks him for hazelnuts! Now where did the hazel trees go?"

Torak hefted Wolf higher in his arms. "The harm you think we bring," he said. "Do you mean—"

"They know what he means," said the Walker. "The bear demon, the demon bear. And the Walker *told* him not to summon it!"

Torak stopped. "Told who? Do you mean—the crippled wanderer? The one who made the bear?"

A jab of the knife reminded him to keep moving. "The crippled one, yes of course! The wise one, always after the demons to do his bidding." Another bark of laughter. "But the Wolf boy doesn't know about demons, does he? Doesn't even know what they are! Ah yes, the Walker can always tell."

Renn looked surprised. Torak avoided her eyes.

"The Walker knows about them," the man went on, still scanning the slopes for hazel trees. "Oh yes. Before the flint bit him, he was a wise man himself. He knew that if you die and lose your name-soul, then you're a ghost, and you forget who you are. The Walker always feels sorry for ghosts. But if you lose your *clan*-soul, then what's left is a demon."

Leaning forward, he engulfed Torak in a blast of

rank breath. "Think about that, Wolf boy. No clan-soul, and you're a demon. The raw power of the Nanuak, but with no clan feeling to tame it; just the rage that something's been taken from you. That's why they hate the living."

Torak knew the Walker was telling the truth. He'd seen that hatred himself. It had killed his father. "What about the crippled one?" he asked hoarsely. "The one who caught the demon and trapped it in the bear? What was his name?"

"Ah," said the Walker, gesturing at Torak to move on. "So *wise*, so *clever*. To start with, he only wants the little demons, the slitherers and the scurriers. But they're never strong enough for him; he always wants more. So then he calls up the biters and the hunters. Still not enough." He grinned, giving Torak another blast of carrion breath. "In the end," he whispered, "he summons—an *elemental*."

Renn gasped.

Torak was mystified. "What's that?"

The Walker laughed. "Ah, she knows! The Raven girl knows!"

Renn met Torak's eyes. Her own were very dark. "The stronger the souls, the stronger the demon." She licked her lips. "An elemental comes into being when something hugely powerful dies—something like a waterfall or an ice river—and its souls are scattered. An elemental is the strongest demon of all."

Wolf wriggled out of Torak's arms and disappeared into the ferns. An elemental, Torak thought dazedly.

But this talk of demons was upsetting the Walker all over again. "Ach, how they hate the living!" he moaned, rocking from side to side. "Too bright, too bright, all the shiny, shiny souls! Hurts! Hurts! It's *their* fault, the Wolf boy and the Raven girl! They bring it with them to the Walker's beautiful valley!"

"But we're nearly out of your valley," said Renn.

"Yes, look," said Torak, "we're nearly at the top—"

The Walker would not be calmed. "Why do they do it?" he shouted. "Why? The Walker never did them any harm!" Brandishing their bows above his head, he gripped them at both ends, as if to break them in two.

That was too much for Renn. "Don't you *dare*!" she shouted. "Don't you *dare* hurt my bow!"

"Back!" roared the Walker. "Or he snaps them like twigs!"

"Put them *down*!" yelled Renn, leaping at him and trying in vain to reach her bow.

Torak had to act fast. Quickly he opened his food pouch, then held out his palm. "Hazelnuts!" he cried. "Hazelnuts for Narik!"

The effect was immediate. "Hazelnuts," murmured the Walker. Dropping their bows on the stones, he snatched the nuts from Torak's hand and squatted on his haunches. Then he pulled a rock from his cape and began cracking them. "Hm, nice and sweet. Narik will be pleased."

Quietly, Renn retrieved the bows and brushed off the wet. She offered Torak his, but he didn't take it. He was staring at the rock that the Walker was using to crack the nuts. "Who is Narik?" he said, eager to keep the Walker talking so that he could get a closer look. "Is he your friend?"

"The Walker can see him plain enough," he muttered. "Why can't the Wolf boy? Something wrong with his eyes?" Plunging his hand into his cape, he drew out a mangy brown mouse. It was clutching half a hazelnut in its paws and looked up peevishly at being interrupted.

Torak blinked. The mouse sneezed and went back to its meal.

Tenderly, the Walker stroked the small, humped back with his grimy finger. "Ah, the Walker's fosterling."

The rock lay discarded on the ground. It was about the size of Torak's hand: a sharp, curved claw—made of gleaming black stone.

Where there's a stone claw, might there also be a stone tooth? Torak glanced at Renn. She'd seen it too. And from her expression, she'd had the same thought. *Oldest of all, the stone bite.* The second part of the Nanuak.

"That stone," Torak said carefully. "Would the Walker tell me where he got it?"

The Walker raised his head, dazed from stroking his mouse. Then his face convulsed. "Stone mouth," he said. "Long time, bad time. He's hiding. Otters have thrown him out, but he's not yet found his beautiful valley."

Again Torak and Renn exchanged glances. Did they dare risk another outburst?

"The stone creature," said Torak. "Does it have stone teeth inside the stone mouth?"

"Of course!" snarled the Walker, "or how could it eat?"

"Where can we find it?" asked Renn.

"The Walker *said*! In the stone mouth!"

"And where is the creature with the stone mouth?"

Suddenly, the Walker's face went slack, and he looked very tired. "Bad place," he whispered. "Very bad. The killing earth that gulps and swallows. The Watchers everywhere. They see you, but you don't see them. Not till it's too late."

"Tell us how to find it," said Torak.

NINETEEN

"How can you have a stone creature, anyway?" said Renn crossly. She'd been in a bad mood ever since losing her quiver.

"I don't know," said Torak for the tenth time.

"And what kind of creature? Boar? Lynx? We should've asked."

"He probably wouldn't have told us."

Renn put her hands on her hips, shaking her head. "We've done everything he said. We've walked for two whole days. Crossed three valleys. Followed the stream he mentioned. Still nothing. I think he was just trying to get rid of us."

The same thought had occurred to Torak, but he wasn't going to admit it. In two days, the fog hadn't lifted. It felt wrong. Everything about this place felt wrong.

After some persuasion, the Walker had returned the rest of their weapons and sent them on their way. Following the Walker's directions, they'd left the "stream at the foot of the stony gray hill," and were climbing the trail that snaked toward the top. It had a bleak, menacing feel. Stunted birches loomed out of the fog. Here and there they saw the gleam of naked rock, where the hill had been rubbed raw. The only sound was the hammer-like *chack-chack* of a woodpecker warning rivals away.

"He doesn't want us here," said Renn. "Maybe we've come the wrong way."

"If we had, Wolf would have told us."

Renn looked doubtful. "Do you still believe that?"

"Yes," said Torak, "I do. After all, if he hadn't led us to the Walker's valley, we wouldn't have seen the stone claw, and then we wouldn't have known anything about a stone tooth."

"Maybe. But I still think we've come too far east. We're getting too close to the High Mountains."

"How can you tell, when we can't see ten paces ahead?"

"I can feel it. That freezing air? It's coming off the ice river."

Torak stopped and stared at her. "What ice river?"

"The one at the foot of the High Mountains."

Torak set his teeth. He was getting tired of being the one who didn't know things.

They climbed on in silence, and soon even the woodpecker was left behind. Torak became uneasily aware of the noise they were making: the creak of his pack, the rattle of pebbles as Renn struggled ahead. He could feel the rocks listening, the twisted trees silently warning him back.

Suddenly, Renn turned and clattered down toward him. "We got it wrong!" she panted, her eyes wide and scared.

"What do you mean?"

"The Walker never said it was a stone *creature*! *We* were the ones who said that. He only ever said it was a stone *mouth*!" Grabbing his arm, she dragged him up the hill.

The ground leveled out and the trail ended. Torak came to a dead halt in the swirling fog. As he took in what lay ahead, dread settled inside him.

A rock face towered above them, gray as a thundercloud. At its foot, guarded by a solitary yew tree, was a cavern of darkness like a silent scream: a gaping stone mouth.

"We can't go in there," said Renn.

"We—I—have to," said Torak. "This is the stone

mouth the Walker was talking about. It's where he found the stone claw. It's where I might find the stone tooth."

Close up, the cave mouth was smaller than he'd first thought: a shadowy half circle no higher than his shoulder. He put his hand on the stone lip and bent to peer inside.

"Be careful," warned Renn.

The cave floor sloped away steeply. Cold flowed from it: an acrid uprush of air like the breath of some ancient creature that has never seen the sun.

"Bad place," the Walker had said. "Very bad. The killing earth that gulps and swallows. The Watchers everywhere."

"Don't move your hand," said Renn beside him.

Glancing up, he saw with a start that his fingers were a hair's breadth away from a large splayed hand that had been hammer-etched deep into the stone. He snatched his own away.

"It's a warning," whispered Renn. "You see the three bars above the middle finger? Those are lines of power, warding off evil." She leaned closer. "It's old. Very old. We can't go in. There's something down there."

"What?" asked Torak. "What's down there?"

She shook her head. "I don't know. Maybe a doorway to the Otherworld. It must be bad, for someone to have carved that hand."

Torak thought about that. "I don't think I have a choice. I'll go. You stay here."

"No! If you go, I'm going too—"

"Wolf can't come with me; he couldn't take the smell. You stay here with him. If I need help, I'll call."

It took a while, but the more he argued, the more he convinced himself, too.

He got ready by laying his bow and quiver under the yew tree along with his pack, sleeping-sack, and water-skin, then unhooking his axe from his belt. Only his knife would be any use in the dark. Finally, he cut a rawhide leash for the cub. Wolf wriggled and snapped until Torak managed to explain that he had to stay with Renn, who settled the matter by producing a handful of dried lingonberries from her food pouch. But Torak couldn't find a way to tell Wolf that he'd be coming back. Wolf talk didn't seem to deal with the future.

Renn gave him a sprig of rowan for protection, and one of her salmon-skin mittens on a cord. "Remember," she said, "if you find the stone tooth, don't touch it with your bare hands. And you'd better let me have the pouch with the river eyes."

She was right. There was no telling what might happen if he took the Nanuak into the cave.

With an odd sense of giving up an unwelcome burden, Torak handed her the raven-skin pouch, and she tied it to her belt. Wolf watched what was happening with ears swiveling: as if, thought Torak, the pouch was making some kind of noise.

"You'll need light," said Renn, glad to be doing something practical. From her pack she brought out two rushlights: the peeled pith of rushes that had been soaked in deer fat, then dried in the sun. With her strike-fire, she lit a curl of juniper bark tinder, and one of the rushlights flared into life: a bright, clear, comforting flame. Torak felt hugely grateful.

"If you need help," she said, kneeling and hugging Wolf to stop herself shivering, "shout. We'll come running."

Torak nodded. Then he stooped and entered the stone mouth.

He groped for the wall. It felt slimy, like dead flesh.

He shuffled forward, feeling the way with his feet. The rushlight trembled and shrank to a glimmer. The stench wafted up from the darkness, stinging his nostrils.

After several halting steps, he came up against stone. The cave mouth had narrowed to a gullet: He'd have to turn sideways to get through. Shutting his eyes, he edged in. It felt as if he was being swallowed. He couldn't breathe. He kept thinking of the weight of the rock pressing in on him. . . .

The air cooled. He was still in a tunnel, but it was

wider, and twisted sharply to the right. Glancing back, he saw that the daylight had vanished, and with it Renn and Wolf.

The stink got stronger as he followed the tunnel, hearing nothing but his own breathing, seeing nothing but glimpses of glistening red stone.

A sudden chill to his left, and he nearly lost his footing. Pebbles rattled, then dropped into silence.

The left-hand wall had vanished. He was standing on a narrow ledge jutting out over darkness. From far below came an echoing *plink* of water. One slip and he'd be over the edge.

Another bend—this time to the left—and a rock beneath his foot tilted. With a cry he grabbed for a handhold, righting himself just in time.

At the sound of his cry, something stirred.

He froze.

"Torak?" Renn's voice sounded far away.

He didn't dare call out. Whatever had moved had gone still again: but it was a horrible, waiting stillness. It knew he was there. *The Watchers everywhere. They see you, but you don't see them. Not till it's too late.*

He forced himself to go on. Down, always down. The stink came at him in waves. *Breathe through your mouth,* said a voice in his head. That was what he and Fa used to do when they came upon a stinking kill site or a bat-infested cave. He tried it, and the stench became bearable, although it still caught at his eyes and throat.

Abruptly the ground leveled out, and he felt space opening up around him. A dim light had to be coming from somewhere, because he made out a vast, shadowy cavern. The fumes were almost overwhelming. He was in the dripping, reeking bowels of the earth.

The ledge he was standing on ended, and the floor beyond it was weirdly humped. In the middle of the cavern, a great, flat-topped stone gleamed like black ice. It looked as if it had stood untouched for thousands of winters. Even from twenty paces away, Torak could feel its power.

This was where the Walker had found his stone claw. This was the reason for the warning hand at the cave mouth. This was what the Watchers guarded: a door to the Otherworld.

Torak couldn't take another step. It was like the times when he awoke so heavy with sleep that to stir even a finger seemed impossible.

To steady himself, he put his free hand on the hilt of his knife. The sinew binding felt faintly warm, giving him the courage to step down onto the cave floor.

As he did, he cried out in disgust. The floor sank beneath his boot: a noisome softness sucking him down. *The killing earth that gulps and swallows.*

His cry rang round the walls, and far above him he

heard a stealthy movement. Something dark detached itself from the roof and swooped toward him.

There was nowhere to hide, nowhere to run. The softness sucked at his boots like wet sand. A fetid downrush, and the thing was on him: greasy fur clogging his mouth and nose, sharp claws tearing at his hair. Snarling with horror, he beat at the silent attacker.

At last it lifted away with a leathery *thwap*. But he knew that it wasn't vanquished. The Watcher had merely come to find out what he was. Once it knew, it had left.

But what was it? A bat? A demon? How many more were there?

Torak floundered on. Halfway to the stone, he stumbled and fell. The stink was unbearable. He wallowed in choking blackness, he couldn't see, couldn't think. Even the rushlight turned black—a black flame flaring above him. . . .

He staggered to his feet, shaking himself free like a swimmer gasping for air. His mind steadied. The black flame burned yellow again.

He reached the stone. On its ancient smoothness, six stone claws had been arranged in a spiral, with a gap where the Walker had snatched the seventh. At the center lay a single black stone tooth.

Oldest of all, the stone bite. The second part of the Nanuak.

Sweat slid down his spine. He wondered what power he would unleash if he touched it.

He stretched out his hand, then snatched it back, remembering Renn's warning. "Don't touch the Nanuak with your bare hands."

Where was the mitten? He must have dropped it.

With the rushlight he cast around, plunging his hand into the stinking mounds. Again the dizziness mounted. Again the flame darkened. . . .

Just in time, he found the mitten, tied to his belt. Yanking it on, he reached for the tooth.

The rushlight glimmered on the cave wall behind the stone—and lit the gleam of thousands of eyes.

With his hand poised above the tooth, he moved the flame slowly to and fro. It caught the liquid gleam of eyes. The walls were swarming with Watchers. Wherever the light touched, they rippled and heaved like a maggot-riddled carcass. If he took the tooth, they would come for him.

Suddenly, everything happened at once.

From far above came Wolf's sharp, urgent bark.

Renn screamed, "Torak! It's coming!"

The Watchers exploded around him.

The rushlight went out.

Something struck him in the back and he fell forward onto the stone.

Again Renn screamed. "Torak! *The bear!*"

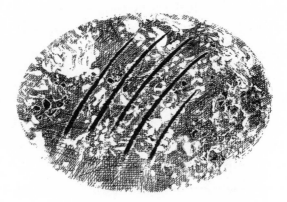

TWENTY

Clutching Torak's quiver, Renn raced to the edge of the trail and tripped on a tree root, spilling arrows in the dirt. Panic bubbled in her throat. What to do? What to *do*?

Only moments before, she'd been pacing up and down, while a flock of greenfinches tore at the yew tree's juicy pink berries and Wolf tugged on the leash, uttering bark-growls that Torak would have understood, but she just found worrying.

Then the finches had fled in a twittering cloud, and she'd glanced down the hill. A gap in the fog had given her a clear view: She'd seen the stream rushing past a clump of spruce, and a big dark boulder hunched beside them. Then the boulder had moved.

Frozen in horror, she'd watched the bear rear up on its hind legs, towering over the spruce. The great head swung as it tasted the air. It caught her scent and dropped to all fours.

That was when she'd run to the cave and screamed a warning to Torak—and got nothing back but echoes.

Now, as the fog closed in again and she fumbled for the arrows, she pictured the bear climbing the hill toward her. She knew how fast bears can move: it would be here in moments.

The rock face was too steep for her to climb; besides, she couldn't leave Wolf. That left the cave, but every part of her screamed not to go inside. They'd be caught like hares in a trap; they'd never get out.

Wolf's desperate tugging on the leash broke her panic. He was pulling her toward the cave—and in a flash she knew he was right. Torak was inside. They would fight it together.

She plunged in, dragging packs and sleeping-sacks behind her. The darkness blinded her. She ran into solid rock, hitting her head.

After a breathless search, she worked out that the cave narrowed sharply to a slit. Wolf was already through, pulling at her to follow. She turned and edged sideways—quickly, quickly—then dropped to her knees and reached through the gap to drag the gear in after her.

As she yanked in packs and bows and quiver, she felt a flicker of hope. Maybe the gap was too narrow for the bear? Maybe they could hold out. . . .

Her waterskin was wrenched from her hand with a force that slammed her against the gap and sent pain shooting through her shoulder. In a daze she scrambled sideways into a hollow, yanking Wolf with her.

The bear couldn't have moved that fast, she thought numbly.

A deep growl reverberated through the cave. Her skin crawled.

It can't get through the gap, she told herself. Stay still. Stay very, very still.

From deep within the cave came a cry. "Renn!"

Was Torak calling for help, or was he coming to help her? She couldn't tell. Couldn't call out. Couldn't do anything but cower with Wolf in the hollow, knowing she was too close to the gap—just two paces away—yet powerless to move. Some force was keeping her there. She couldn't take her eyes from that narrow slit of daylight.

The daylight turned black.

Knowing it was the worst thing to do, Renn leaned forward and peered through the gap. The blood roared in her head. A nightmare glimpse of dark fur flickering in an unfelt wind; a flash of long cruel claws glistening with black blood.

A roar shook the cave. Moaning, Renn jammed her fists against her ears as the roar battered through her, on and on till she thought her skull would crack. . . .

Silence: as shocking as the roar. Taking her fists from her ears, she heard a whisper of dust. Wolf panting. Nothing else.

Slowly, appalled at what she was doing, she crawled toward the slit, pulling the reluctant cub with her.

She saw daylight again. Gray rock face. The yew tree with a scattering of berries beneath. No bear.

A shuddering growl, so close that she heard the wet champ of jaws, smelled the reek of slaughter. Then the daylight was blotted out, and an eye held hers. Blacker than basalt, yet churning with fire, it drew her—it *wanted* her.

She tilted forward.

Wolf wrenched her back, breaking the spell so that she shrank out of the way just as the deadly claws sliced the earth where she'd been kneeling.

Again the bear roared. Again she cowered in the hollow. Then she heard new sounds: the clatter of rocks, the groans of a dying tree. In its fury, the bear was clawing at the mouth of the cave, uprooting the yew and tearing it apart.

Whimpering, she pressed herself into the hollow.

Against her shoulder, the rock moved. With a cry she jumped back.

From the other side, she heard stones shattering, and earth being flung aside with lethal intent. She realized what was happening. The rock that formed this side of the gap was not, as she had thought, a part of the cave itself, but merely a tongue of stone that jutted from the earth floor. The bear was clawing at its roots: digging them out like wood ants from a nest.

Sweat streamed off her. She stared at Wolf.

With a shock, she saw that he was a cub no longer. His head was down, his eyes fixed on the thing beyond the slit. His black lips were peeled back in a snarl, baring formidable white fangs.

Something hardened inside her. "Not like wood ants," she whispered. The sound of her voice gave her courage.

She untied the leash to give Wolf his freedom: Maybe he could escape, even if she and Torak could not. Then she groped for her bow. The touch of the cool, smooth yew gave her strength. She got to her feet.

Concentrate on the target, she told herself, remembering the many lessons Fin-Kedinn had given her. That's the most important thing. You must concentrate so hard that you burn a hole in the target. . . . And keep your draw arm relaxed; don't tense up. The force comes from your back, not from your arm. . . .

"Fourteen arrows," she said. "I should be able to put in a few of them before it gets me."

She stepped out from the hollow and took up her position.

Torak tore at the Watchers swarming over him.

Claws snagged his face and hair. Foul wings stifled his mouth and nose. Somehow he managed to pull on Renn's mitten and pick up the stone tooth. It was heavier than he'd expected. He wrenched off the mitten with the tooth inside, and shoved it into the neck of his jerkin.

"Renn!" he yelled as he pushed himself off the stone. His cry was deadened by leathery wings.

He struck out through the stench—but with the rushlight gone, he couldn't even see his hands in front of his face.

Faint and far above came Wolf's frenzied yowls: *Where are you? Danger! Danger!*

He waded toward the sound with the Watchers swarming over him, pushing him down into the stink.

Terrible images filled his head. Wolf and Renn lying dead—just like Fa. *Why* had he made them stay up there where it was "safe," when all the time that was where the true danger lay?

Raging inwardly, he drew his knife from its sheath and slashed at the Watchers. They seemed to lift to avoid the blade. "Oh, so you're scared of it, are you?" he shouted. "Well, here's some more!" He slashed at them—and again they lifted, a dark cloud just out of reach. The hilt grew hot in his hand. Snarling, he plowed on through the stink.

He barked his shins on solid rock. He'd reached the ledge. "I'm coming!" he shouted, pulling himself out and starting up the slope.

A roar shook the cave, beating him to his knees. The Watchers rose in a cloud and vanished.

The silence after the last echo had died was worse. Torak became aware of rock beneath his knees; the stone tooth throbbing inside his jerkin. He struggled to his feet and ran up the ledge. It was steep—so steep. Why was there no sound from above? What was happening up there?

On and on he climbed till his knees ached and the breath seared his throat. Then he rounded the last bend and the daylight blinded him.

The cave mouth was five paces away, and wider than he remembered. The gap he'd squeezed through on his descent had been wrenched open, and before it stood Renn, a small, upright figure, incredibly brave, taking aim with her last arrow at the thing looming over her.

For a heartbeat, Torak was back with Fa on the night of the attack, transfixed by the malice of those demon-haunted eyes. . . .

"No!" he shouted.

Renn loosed her arrow. The bear batted it away with one sweep of its claws. But just as it was about to move in for the kill, Wolf leaped from the shadows—leaped not at the bear, but at Renn. With a single snap of his powerful jaws, Wolf tore the raven-skin pouch from her belt—knocking her off her feet, out of reach of the bear—then sped out of the cave. The bear lashed out, gouging the earth a hand's breadth from where the cub had been.

"Wolf!" shouted Torak, throwing himself forward.

With the pouch in his jaws, Wolf disappeared into the fog. The bear swung around with terrifying agility and raced after him.

"Wolf!" Torak shouted again.

The fog engulfed them, leaving the empty hillside mocking him. The bear was gone. So was Wolf.

TWENTY-ONE

Where are you? Torak's desolate howl echoed off the rockface.

Where are you? the hills howled back at him.

The old pain was opening up in his chest. First Fa, now Wolf. Please, not Wolf . . .

Renn stood blinking at the mouth of the cave.

"*Why* did you let him off the leash?" he cried.

She swayed. "I had to. Had to set him free."

With a cry, Torak started rooting around in the wreckage.

"What are you doing?" said Renn.

"Looking for my pack. I'm going after Wolf."

"But it'll be dark soon!"

"So we just sit here and wait?"

"No! We salvage our gear; we build a shelter and a fire. *Then* we wait. We wait for Wolf to find us."

Torak bit back a retort. For the first time, he noticed that Renn was shaking. She had a bloody scrape down one cheek, and a bruise the size of a pigeon's egg coming up over the other eye.

He felt ashamed. She'd faced the bear. She'd even had the courage to shoot at it. He shouldn't have shouted. "I'm sorry," he said. "I didn't mean . . . You're right. I can't track him in the dark."

Renn sat down heavily on a boulder. "I had no idea what it would be like," she said. "I never thought it would be so . . ." She covered her mouth with both hands.

Torak unearthed an arrow from the rubble. The shaft was snapped in two. "Did you hit it?" he asked.

"I don't know. I don't think it matters. Arrows can't bring it down." She shook her head. "One moment it was after me, and the next it was after Wolf. Why?"

He tossed away the broken arrow shaft. "Does that matter?"

"Maybe." She glanced at him. "Did you get the stone tooth?"

He'd almost forgotten about it. Now, as he reached inside his jerkin and brought out the mitten, he just wanted to be rid of it. Because of the Nanuak, Wolf might be dead. No more grooming nibbles in the morning; no more uproarious games of hide and hunt . . . Torak bit his knuckle, fighting his fear. He couldn't lose Wolf.

Renn took the mitten and turned it in her fingers. "We've got the second part of the Nanuak," she said thoughtfully, "and lost the first. But why did Wolf take it?"

With an effort, Torak forced his mind to what she was saying. Something flickered in his memory. "Do you remember," he said, "when I found the river eyes—it was as if Wolf could hear them. Or sense them in some way."

Renn frowned. "You think—the bear can too?"

"'All the shiny shiny souls,'" he murmured. "That's what the Walker said. Demons hate the living; they hate the brightness of the souls."

"And if the souls of ordinary creatures are too bright," said Renn, getting to her feet and beginning to pace, "then how much brighter—more dazzling—must the Nanuak be!"

"That's why it attacked you—because you had the river eyes—"

"And that's why Wolf took the pouch. Because he *knew*. Because—" She stopped pacing and stared at Torak. "Because he was luring the bear away from us.

Oh, Torak. He saved our lives."

Torak stumbled to the edge of the trail. The fog was clearing at last, and below him, the vastness of the Forest marched away into the west. What chance did Wolf have out there, alone against the bear?

"Wolves are cleverer than bears," said Renn.

"He's just a cub, Renn. He's not even four moons old."

"But he's also the guide. If anyone can find a way, he can."

Wolf raced between the beech trees, the wind at his tail and the shining, singing raven skin gripped tight in his jaws.

Far away, he heard the lonely howl of Tall Tailless.

Wolf longed to howl back, but he couldn't. The wind was gusting the demon's scent toward him. He smelled its rage and its terrible hunger; he heard its tireless breath. Strongest of all, he sensed its hatred: hatred for him and for the thing he bore.

But Wolf knew with a fierce, bright joy that it would never catch him. The demon was fast, but he was faster.

He no longer felt like a cub who must wait for the poor, slow taillesses to catch up. He was a *wolf*—racing between the trees in the swift wolf-lope that goes on forever. He reveled in the strength of his legs and the stretch of his back; in the suppleness that let him turn at full speed on a single paw. Oh no, the demon would never catch him!

Wolf paused to drink at a noisy little Wet, dropping the raven skin for a moment. Then he snatched it up and settled back into his stride, climbing higher toward the Great White Cold that he'd only ever smelled in his sleeps.

A fresh scent drove that from his head: he was entering the range of a pack of stranger wolves. Every few paces, he passed their scent markings. He must be careful. If they caught him, they might attack. When he needed to spill his scent, he waited till he reached another little Fast Wet and spilled into that, instead of marking a tree. His scent would wash away, and neither the stranger wolves nor the demon would smell him.

The Dark came. Wolf loved the Dark. In it, smells and sounds were sharper, but he could see almost as well as in the Light.

Far ahead, the stranger pack began its evening howl. That made Wolf sad. He remembered how joyfully his pack used to howl; how keenly they greeted each other after their sleeps. The snuffle-licking and the rubbing of scents against each other; the smiling and playing as they encouraged one another for the hunt.

Quite suddenly, as Wolf thought of his pack, he

began to tire. He felt each pad strike the rocks as never before. He felt an ache running up his legs. He began to hurt.

Fear gnawed at him. He could not go on forever. He could not go on much farther at all. He was far from Tall Tailless, and crossing the range of a stranger pack. And the demon was tracking him relentlessly through the Dark.

Torak dragged what remained of their gear into the yew branch shelter, then kicked at the fire, sending sparks shooting skyward. This waiting was terrible. He'd been howling since dusk. He knew that he risked drawing the bear, but Wolf was more important. Where was he?

It was a cold, starry night, and even without looking up, he could feel the red eye of the Great Auroch glaring down at him. Relishing his turmoil.

Renn emerged from the darkness, bearing an armful of leaves and bark.

"You were a long time," Torak said curtly.

"I needed the right things. No sign of Wolf?"

He shook his head.

Renn knelt by the fire and tipped her load onto the ground. "When I was looking for these, I heard horns. Birch-bark horns."

Torak was horrified. "What? Where?"

She nodded toward the west. "Long way away."

"Was it—Fin-Kedinn?"

Again she nodded.

Torak shut his eyes. "I thought he'd have given up by now."

"He doesn't give up," said Renn. There was a hint of pride in her voice, which irritated him.

"Have you forgotten," he said, "that he wanted to kill me? *The Listener gives his heart's blood to the Mountain*'?"

She rounded on him. "Of course I haven't forgotten! But I'm worried about them! If the bear isn't up here, then it's down there, where they are. Why else would Fin-Kedinn blow the horn?"

Torak felt bad. Renn was worried, and so was he. Fighting didn't help.

From his belt he untied the little grouse-bone whistle he'd made when he'd first found Wolf. "Here." He held it out. "Now you can call Wolf too."

She looked at him in surprise. "Thanks."

There was a silence. Torak asked her why she needed the herbs.

"For the stone tooth. We've got to find some way of hiding it from the bear. If we don't, it'll track us down."

Like it's tracking Wolf, thought Torak. The ache in his chest deepened. "If the rowan leaves and the pouch couldn't hide the river eyes," he said, "why do you think bark and wormwood can do any better?"

"Because I'm going to use them for something stronger." She chewed her lip. "I've been trying to remember exactly what Saeunn does. She's always trying to teach me Magecraft, and I'm always going hunting instead. I wish I'd listened."

"You're lucky there's something you can do," muttered Torak.

"But what if I get it wrong?"

He didn't answer. He could feel the red eye mocking him. Even if Wolf did find a way back, he'd be bringing the bear with him, drawn by the river eyes. And the only way Wolf could shake off the bear would be by losing the river eyes—which would mean there'd be no chance of destroying the bear.

There had to be a way out, but Torak couldn't see it.

Wolf was tiring fast. There was no way out.

By now, the demon had fallen too far behind to be able to sense the raven skin, but it was still tracking him by scent, and it would go on tracking him. When at last he slowed, as his aching paws longed to, it would catch him.

The stranger pack had long since ended their howl and gone hunting, far away in the Mountains. Wolf missed their voices. He felt truly alone.

The wind turned, and he caught a new scent. Reindeer. Wolf had never hunted reindeer, but he knew the scent well, for his mother used to bring him the branches that grow from reindeers' heads, with the hide hanging off in delicious, chewable tatters. Now, as he smelled the herd in the next valley, the blood urge put new strength in his limbs, and hope leaped within him. If he could reach them . . .

As he heaved himself up the slope, the thunder of many hooves drew nearer. Suddenly the great prey burst upon him, galloping with their branched heads high and their huge hooves splayed, as they flowed between the beech trees like an unstoppable Fast Wet.

Wolf turned on one paw and leaped among them, and they towered over him as he plunged into their musky scent. A bull charged, and Wolf dodged the head-branches. A cow snorted at him to stay away from her calf, and he ducked beneath her to escape her pounding hooves. But soon the herd sensed that he wasn't hunting them, and forgot about him. He ran up the valley, his scent swallowed up by that of the herd.

They left the beeches and ran through a spruce forest. The rocks became bigger, the trees smaller; then the trees were left behind entirely as they streamed out onto a stony flatness like nothing he'd ever known.

By the smell on the wind, Wolf knew this flatness stretched for many lopes into the Dark, and that beyond it lay the Great White Cold. What was it? He didn't know. But somewhere beyond lay the thing that had called to him from his first Den, pulling him on. . . .

Far behind him, the demon bellowed. It had lost his scent! In delight, Wolf tossed the raven skin high in the air and caught it with a snap.

After a time, another noise reached him. Very faint, but unmistakable: the high, flat call that Tall Tailless made when he put the bird bone to his muzzle!

Then another, even more beloved sound: Tall Tailless himself, howling for him! The best sound in the Forest!

The reindeer ran on, but Wolf knew that he had to turn back and head into the Forest again. It was not yet time to reach the Great White Cold and what lay beyond; he had to go back and fetch Tall Tailless.

TWENTY-TWO

Renn was huddled in her sleeping-sack, thinking about getting up, when Torak appeared at the entrance to the shelter, making her jump.

"Time we got started," he said, crouching by the fire and handing her a strip of dried deer meat. From the shadows under his eyes, she guessed that he hadn't slept any better than she had.

She sat up and took a halfhearted bite of her daymeal. The scrape on her cheek felt hot, and the bruise above her eye hurt. But worse than that was the creeping dread. It wasn't only the nearness of the cave, or terror of the bear. It was something else: something she didn't want to think about.

"I found the trail," said Torak, cutting across her thoughts.

She stopped in mid chew. "Which way did they go?"

"West, around the other side of the hill, then down into a beech wood." He reached out and stirred the fire, his thin face sharp with anxiety. "The bear was right behind him."

Renn pictured Wolf racing through the Forest with the bear closing in. "Torak," she said, "you do realize that when we track Wolf, we'll also be tracking the bear?"

"Yes."

"If we catch up with it—"

"I know," he broke in, "but I'm sick of waiting. We've waited all night, and still nothing. We've got to go and find him. At least, I've got to. You can stay here—"

"No! Of course I'm coming with you! I was only saying." She looked at the salmon-skin mitten hanging from the roof post.

"Do you think it'll work?" said Torak, following her gaze.

"I don't know."

The charm had sounded so clever when she'd explained it to him yesterday. "When someone gets ill," she'd said, feeling quite important, "it's usually because they've eaten something bad. But sometimes it's because their souls have been lured away by demons. The sick souls need to be rescued. I've seen Saeunn do it lots of times. She ties little fishhooks to her fingertips to help her catch the sick souls; then she takes a special potion to loosen her own souls, so that they can leave her body and find the—"

"What's this got to do with the Nanuak?"

"I'm *about* to tell you," she'd said with a quelling look. "To find them, Saeunn has to hide her *own* souls from the demons."

"Ah. So if you do what she does, you can hide the Nanuak from the bear?"

"I think so, yes. To disguise herself, she smears her face with wormwood and earthblood, then puts on a mask of rowan bark tied with hairs from each member of the clan. That's what I'm going to do. Well, in a way."

After that, she'd made a little box of folded rowan bark and smeared it with wormwood and red ochre. Then she'd put the stone tooth inside and tied it up with locks of her own and Torak's hair.

It had been a relief to be doing something instead of worrying about Wolf, and she'd felt proud of herself. But now, in the freezing dawn, doubts crowded in. After all, what did she know about Magecraft?

"Come on," said Torak, jumping up. "The tracking's

good. Light's nice and low."

Renn peered out of the shelter. "What about the bear? It might have lost Wolf's scent and be coming back for us."

"I don't think so," he said. "I think it's still after Wolf."

Somehow, that didn't make her feel any better.

"What's wrong?" said Torak.

She sighed. What she wanted to say was: "I'm really, *really* missing my clan; I'm terrified that Fin-Kedinn will never forgive me for helping you escape; I think we're mad to be deliberately tracking the bear; I've got a horrible feeling that we're going to end up at the one place I don't ever want to go; and I'm worried that I shouldn't even *be* here, because unlike you, I'm not the Listener and I'm not in the Prophecy, I'm just Renn. But it's no use saying any of this, because all you can think about is finding Wolf." So in the end she simply said, "Nothing. Nothing's wrong."

Torak threw her a disbelieving look and started stamping out the fire.

All morning, they followed the trail through the beech wood and then through a spruce forest, turning north-east and steadily climbing. As always, Renn was unsettled by Torak's skill at tracking. He seemed to go into a trance, scanning the land with endless patience and often finding some tiny sign that most full-grown hunters would have missed.

It was midafternoon and the light was beginning to fail when he stopped.

"What is it?" asked Renn.

"Sh! I thought I heard something." He cupped his hand to his ear. "There! Do you hear it?"

She shook her head.

His face broke into a grin. "It's Wolf!"

"Are you sure?"

"I'd know his howl anywhere. Come on, he's up that way!" He pointed east.

Renn's heart sank. Not east, she thought. Please not east.

As Torak followed the sound, the ground got stonier, and the trees shrank to waist-high birch and willow.

"Are you sure he's here?" said Renn. "If we keep going, we'll end up on the fells."

Torak hadn't heard her; he was running ahead. He disappeared behind a boulder, and a few moments later she heard him excitedly yelling her name.

She raced up the slope and rounded the boulder into the teeth of an icy north wind. She staggered back. They had reached the very edge of the Forest. The edge of the fells.

Before her stretched a vast treeless waste, where

heather and dwarf willow hugged the ground in a vain attempt to avoid the wind; where small peat-brown lakes shivered amid tossing marsh grass. Far in the distance, a treacherous scree slope towered above the fells, and beyond it rose the High Mountains. But between the scree slope and the Mountains, glimpsed only as a white glitter, lay what Renn had been dreading.

Torak, of course, was unaware of all that. "Renn!" he shouted, the wind whipping his voice away. "Over here!"

Dragging her gaze back, she saw that he was kneeling on the bank of a narrow stream. Wolf lay beside him, eyes closed, the raven-skin pouch at his head.

"He's alive!" cried Torak, burying his face in the wet gray fur. Wolf opened one eye and feebly thumped his tail. Renn stumbled through the heather toward them.

"He's exhausted," said Torak without looking up, "and soaking wet. He's been running in the stream to throw the bear off the scent. That was clever, wasn't it?"

Renn glanced around her fearfully. "But did it work?"

"Oh yes," said Torak. "Look at all the marsh pipits. They wouldn't be here if the bear was near."

Wishing she could share his confidence, Renn knelt

and fumbled in her pack for a salmon cake to give to
Wolf. She was rewarded with another, slightly stronger,
tail thump.

It was wonderful to see Wolf again, but she felt
oddly cut off. Too much else was crowding in on her;
too much that Torak didn't know about.

She picked up the raven-skin pouch and loosened
its neck to check inside. The river eyes were still in
their nest of rowan leaves.

"Yes, take it," said Torak, lifting Wolf in his arms
and laying him gently on a patch of soft marsh grass.
"We need to hide it from the bear right away."

Renn untied the rowan-bark box that held the stone
tooth and tipped in the river eyes; then she refastened
the box, put it back in the pouch, and tied it to her belt.

"He'll be all right now," said Torak, stooping to give
the cub's muzzle an affectionate lick. "We can make a
shelter over there in the lee of that slope. Build a fire,
let him rest."

"Not here," said Renn quickly. "We should get back
to the Forest." Out on this windswept fell, she felt
exposed, like a caterpillar dangling on a thread.

"Better if we stay here," said Torak. He pointed
north toward the scree slope and the white glitter.
"That's the fastest way to the Mountain."

Renn's belly tightened. "What? What are you talking about?"

"Wolf told me. That's where we've got to go."

"But—we can't go up there."

"Why not?"

"Because that's the ice river!"

Torak and Wolf looked at her in surprise, and she found herself facing two pairs of wolf eyes: one amber, one light gray. It made her feel very left out.

"But Renn," said Torak patiently, "that's the shortest way to the Mountain."

"I don't care!" She tried to think up some reason that he'd accept. "We've still got to find the third piece of the Nanuak, remember? *'Coldest of all, the darkest light.'* We're not going to find it up there, are we? It'll be cold all right, but there's nothing up there!" Nothing but death, she added to herself.

"You saw the red eye last night," said Torak. "It's getting higher. We've only got a few days—"

"Aren't you listening?" she shouted. "We cannot cross the ice river!"

"Yes we can," he replied with terrifying calm. "We'll find a way."

"How? We've got one waterskin between us and no arrows left! *No arrows!* And it's freezing out there, and you've got only summer clothes!"

He looked at her thoughtfully. "That's not why you don't want to go."

She leaped to her feet and stalked off, then marched

back again. "My father died on an ice river just like that one."

The wind hissed sadly over the fells. Torak looked down at Wolf, then back to her.

"It was a snowfall," she said. "He was on the ice river beyond Lake Axehead. Half an ice cliff came down on him. They didn't find his body till the spring. Saeunn had to do a special rite to get his souls together."

"I'm sorry," said Torak. "I didn't—"

"I'm not telling you so that you'll be sorry for me," she cut in. "I'm telling you so that you'll understand. He was a strong, experienced hunter who *knew* the mountains—and still the ice river killed him. What hope—what chance—do you think we'd have?"

TWENTY-THREE

"Be very, *very* quiet," whispered Renn. "Any sudden noise and it might wake up."

Torak craned his neck at the ice cliffs towering over them. He'd seen ice before, but nothing like this. Not these knife-sharp crags and gaping gullies, these icicles taller than trees. It was as if a great, overarching wave had been frozen by one touch of the World Spirit's finger. And yet, when he'd caught sight of the cliffs from the scree slope, they'd seemed just a wrinkle in the vast, tumbled river of ice.

After letting Wolf rest for a day by the lake, they'd plodded over the marshes and up the scree, where they'd camped in a hollow that had given scant shelter from the wind. There had been no sign of the bear. Perhaps the masking charm had worked; or perhaps, as Renn pointed out, the bear was in the west, wreaking havoc among the clans.

Next morning, they'd climbed the flank of the ice river and started north.

It was madness to walk beneath the ice cliffs when at any moment a snowfall might obliterate them, but they had no choice. The way to the west was blocked by a torrent of meltwater that had carved a deep blue gully.

It was impossible to move quietly. The snow was crisp, and their boots crunched loudly. Torak's new reed cape crackled like dead leaves; even his breath sounded deafening. All around, he heard weird creaks and echoing groans: the ice river murmuring in its sleep. It didn't sound as if it would take much to waken it.

Strangely, that didn't seem to bother Wolf. He *loved* the snow: pouncing on it and tossing lumps of ice high in the air, then skidding to a halt to listen to lemmings and snow voles burrowing under the surface.

Now he stopped to sniff at an ice chunk and patted it with one paw. When it didn't respond, he went down on his forepaws and asked it to play, whining invitingly.

"Sh!" hissed Torak, forgetting to speak wolf.

"Sh!" hissed Renn up ahead.

Desperate to quieten Wolf, Torak pretended to spot some distant prey, by standing very still and staring intently.

Wolf copied him. But when he caught no scent or sound, he twitched his whiskers and glanced at Torak. *Where is it? Where's the prey?*

Torak stretched and yawned. *No prey.*

What? Then why are we hunting?

Just be quiet!

Wolf gave a small, aggrieved whine.

"Come *on!*" whispered Renn. "We've got to get across before nightfall!"

It was freezing in the shadow of the ice cliffs. They'd done what they could while camping by the lake: stuffing their boots with marsh grass, making mittens and caps from Renn's salmon skin and the rest of the rawhide, and the cape for Torak from bunches of reeds tied with marsh grass, then stitched with sinew. But it wasn't nearly enough.

Their supplies were getting low, too: one waterskin and only enough dried salmon and deer meat for a couple of days. Torak could imagine what Fa would say. *A journey in snow is no game, Torak. If you think it is, you'll end up dead.*

He was painfully aware that he didn't actually know much about snow. As Renn had said with her usual unflinching accuracy, "All I know is that it makes tracking a lot easier, it's good for snowballs, and if you get caught in a snowstorm, you're supposed to dig yourself a snow cave and wait till it stops. But that's all I know."

The snow deepened, and soon they were sinking up to their thighs. Wolf dropped behind, cleverly letting Torak break the trail so that he could trot in his footsteps.

"I hope he knows the way," said Renn, keeping her voice down. "I've never been this far north."

"Has anyone?" said Torak.

She raised her eyebrows. "Well, yes. The Ice clans. But they live out on the plains, not on the ice river."

"The Ice clans?"

"The White Foxes. The Ptarmigans. The Narwals. But surely you—"

"No," he said wearily, "I don't. I don't even—"

Behind him, Wolf gave an urgent grunt.

Torak turned to see the cub leaping for cover beneath an arch of solid ice. He glanced up. "Look out!" he cried, grabbing Renn and yanking her under the arch.

An earsplitting crack—and they were overwhelmed by roaring whiteness. Ice thundered around them, smashing into the snow, exploding in lethal shards. Huddled under the arch, Torak prayed that it wouldn't collapse. If it did, they'd be splattered over the snow like crushed lingonberries. . . .

The icefall ended as abruptly as it had begun.

Torak blew out a long breath. Now all he could hear was the soft settling of snow.

"Why did it stop?" hissed Renn.

He shook his head. "Maybe it was just turning over in its sleep."

Renn stared at the ice piled around them. "If it wasn't for Wolf, we'd be under that right now." She was pale, and her clan-tattoos showed up lividly. Torak guessed that she was thinking of her father.

Wolf stood up and shook himself, spattering them with wet snow. He trotted a few paces, took a long sniff, and waited for them to join him.

"Come on," said Torak. "I think it's safe."

"*Safe?*" muttered Renn.

As the day wore on and the sun traveled west through a cloudless sky, puddles of meltwater appeared in the snow, more intensely blue than anything Torak had ever seen. It grew steadily warmer. Around midafternoon, the sun struck the cliffs, and in the blink of an eye, the freezing shadows turned to a stark white glare. Soon Torak was sweating under his reed cape.

"Here," said Renn, handing him a strip of birch bast. "Cut slits in this and tie it around your eyes. Otherwise you'll go snow-blind."

"I thought you'd never been this far north."

"I haven't, but Fin-Kedinn has. He told me about it."

It made Torak uneasy to be peering through a narrow slit when he needed to be on his guard—when every so often a slab of snow or a giant icicle thudded down from the cliffs. As they trudged on, he noticed that Renn was lagging behind. That had never happened before. Usually she was faster than he was.

Waiting for her to catch up, he was startled to see that her lips had a bluish tinge. He asked if she was all right.

She shook her head, bending over with her hands on her knees. "It's been coming on all day," she said. "I feel—drained. I think—I think it's the Nanuak."

Torak felt guilty. He'd been concentrating so hard on not waking the ice river that he'd forgotten that all this time she'd been carrying the raven-skin pouch. "Give it to me," he said. "We'll take turns."

She nodded. "But I'll carry the waterskin. That's only fair."

They swapped. Torak tied the pouch to his belt, while Renn looked over her shoulder at how far they'd come. "Much too slow," she said. "If we don't make it across by nightfall . . ."

She didn't need to add the rest. Torak pictured them digging a snow cave and cowering in darkness, while the ice river heaved and groaned around them.

He said, "Do you think we've got enough firewood?"

Again Renn shook her head.

Before heading for the scree slope, they'd each gathered a faggot of firewood, and prepared a little piece of fire to bring with them. To do this, they'd cut a small chunk of the horsehoof mushroom that grows on dead birch trees, and set fire to it, then blown it out so that it was just smoldering. Then they'd rolled it in birch bark, pierced the bark a few times to let the fire breathe, and plugged the roll with beard-moss to keep it asleep. The fire could be carried all day, slumbering quietly, but ready to be woken with tinder and breath when they needed it.

Torak judged that they had enough firewood to last for maybe a night. If a storm blew up and they had to dig in for days, they would freeze.

They trudged on, and soon Torak understood why the Nanuak had tired Renn. Already he could feel it weighing him down.

Suddenly Renn stopped, yanking the birch bast away from her eyes. "Where's the stream gone?" she breathed.

"What?" said Torak.

"The meltwater! I've just noticed. That gully's gone. Do you think that means we can get out from under the cliffs?"

Taking off his own birch bast, Torak squinted at the

snow. He couldn't see for the glare. "I can still hear it," he said, moving forward to investigate. "Maybe it's just sunk farther under the—"

He got no warning. No crack of ice, no *whump* of collapsing snow. One moment he was walking; the next, he was falling into nothingness.

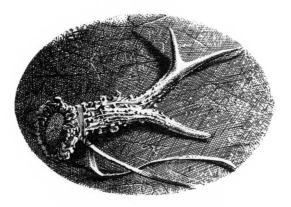

TWENTY-FOUR

Torak jarred his knee so painfully that he cried out.

"Torak!" whispered Renn from above. "Are you all right?"

"I—think so," he replied. But he wasn't. He'd fallen down an ice hole. Only a tiny ledge had stopped him from tumbling to his death.

In the gloom he saw that the hole was narrow—he could touch its sides with his outstretched hands—but fathomless. Far below, he heard the rush of the melt-water torrent. He was *inside* the ice river. How was he going to get out?

Renn and Wolf were peering down at him. They

must be about three paces above. It might as well be thirty. "Now we know where the meltwater went," he said, struggling to stay calm.

"You're not *that* far down," said Renn, trying to encourage him. "At least you've still got your pack."

"And my bow," he replied, hoping he didn't sound too scared. "And the Nanuak." The pouch was still securely tied to his belt. *The Nanuak*, he thought in horror.

What if he couldn't get out? He'd be stuck down here, and the Nanuak would be stuck with him. Without the Nanuak, there would be no chance of destroying the bear. The entire Forest would be doomed: doomed because he hadn't watched his step . . .

"Torak?" whispered Renn. "Are you all right?"

He tried to say yes, but it came out as a croak.

"Not too loud!" breathed Renn. "It might send down another snowfall—or—or close up the hole with you inside. . . ."

"Thanks," he muttered. "I hadn't thought of that."

"Here, try to catch hold of this." Leaning perilously over the edge, she dangled her axe headfirst, with the shaft strap wound around her wrist.

"You couldn't take my weight," he told her. "I'd pull you down; we'd both fall. . . ."

"Fall, fall," echoed the ice around him.

"Is there any way you can climb out?" said Renn,

beginning to sound shaky.

"Probably. If I had the claws of a wolverine."

"Claws, claws," sang the ice.

That gave Torak an idea.

Slowly, terrified of slipping off the ledge, he unhitched his pack from one shoulder and checked that he still had the roe buck antlers. He did. They were short, and their roots had jagged edges. If he could tie one to each wrist and grip the tines, he might be able to use the roots as ice picks to claw his way out.

"What are you going to do?" asked Renn.

"You'll see," he said. He didn't have time to explain. The ledge was getting slippery beneath his boots, and his knee was hurting.

Leaving the antlers in his pack until he needed them, he took his axe from his belt. "I've got to cut notches in the ice," he called to Renn. "I just hope the ice river doesn't feel it."

She did not reply. Of course it would feel it. But what choice did he have?

The first axe blow sent splinters of ice rattling into the chasm. Even if the ice river didn't feel that, it must have heard it.

Clenching his teeth, Torak forced himself to strike another blow. More shards crashed down, the echoes rumbling on and on.

The ice was hard, and he didn't dare swing his

axe for fear of toppling off the ledge, but after much anxious chipping he managed four notches at staggered intervals as high as he could reach, with about a fore-arm's length between each one. They were frighten-ingly shallow—no deeper than his thumb joint—and he had no idea if they'd hold. If he put his weight on one, it might give way, taking him with it.

Shoving his axe back in his belt, he took off his mittens and felt in his pack for the antlers and the last strips of rawhide. His fingers were clumsy with cold, and tying the antlers to his wrists was infuriatingly difficult. At last, using his teeth to tighten the knots, he managed it.

With his right hand he reached for the notch above his head, and dug deep with the jagged edge of the antler. It bit and held. With his left foot, he felt for the first foothold, just a little higher than the ledge. He found it and stepped onto it.

His pack was pulling him backward into the ice hole. Desperately he leaned forward, pressing his face into the ice—and regained his balance.

Wolf yipped at him to hurry. Snow showered down into his hair.

"Stay *back*!" Renn hissed at the cub.

Torak heard sounds of a scuffle—more snow trickled down—then Wolf gave a peevish growl.

"Just a bit farther," said Renn. *"Don't look down."*

Too late. Torak had just done so, and caught a sickening glimpse of the void below.

He reached for the next handhold and missed, snapping off a crust of ice that nearly took him with it. He fought for the handhold—and the antler bit just in time.

Slowly, slowly, he bent his right leg and found the next foothold, about a forearm higher than the one he'd stepped onto with his left. But as he heaved himself onto it, his knee began to shake.

Oh, very clever, Torak, he told himself. You've just put all your weight on the wrong leg—the one you hurt in the fall! "My knee's going," he gasped. "I can't—"

"Yes you can," urged Renn. "Reach for that last handhold, I'll grab you. . . ."

His shoulders were burning; his pack felt as if it was filled with rocks. He gave a huge push and his knee buckled. Then a hand grabbed the shoulder strap of his pack and he was half pulled, half pushed out of the hole.

Torak and Renn lay panting at the edge of the ice hole. Then they heaved themselves up, staggered away from the ice cliffs, and collapsed in a drift of powdery snow. Wolf thought it a huge game, and pranced around them with a big wolf-smile.

Renn gave way to panicky laughter. "That was *far* too close! Next time, look where you're going!"

"I'll try!" panted Torak. He lay on his back, letting the breeze waft snow over his cheeks. High in the sky, thin white clouds were stacking up like petals. He'd never seen anything so beautiful.

Behind him, Wolf was clawing at something in the ice.

"What have you got there?" asked Torak.

But Wolf had freed his prize and was tossing it high and catching it in his jaws, in one of his favorite games. He leaped to catch it in midair, gave it a couple of chews, then bounded over and spat it out on Torak's face. Another favorite game.

"Ow!" said Torak. "Watch what you're doing!" Then he saw what it was. It was about the size of a small fist: brown, furry, and oddly flattened, probably by an icefall. The look of outrage on its little face struck Torak as inexpressibly funny.

"What is it?" said Renn, taking a pull at the water-skin.

He felt laughter welling up inside him. "A frozen lemming."

Renn burst out laughing, spraying water all over the ice.

"Squashed flat," gasped Torak, rolling around in the snow. "You should see its face! So—*surprised*!"

"No, don't!" cried Renn, clutching her sides.

They laughed till it hurt, while Wolf pranced around

with a joyful rocking gait, tossing and catching the frozen lemming. At last he tossed it extravagantly high, made a spectacular twisting leap, and swallowed it in one gulp. Then he decided he was hot, and flopped into a pool of meltwater to cool down.

Renn sat up, wiping her eyes. "Does he ever just *fetch* things, instead of throwing them in your face?"

Torak shook his head. "I've tried asking him. He never does."

He got to his feet. It was turning colder. The wind had strengthened, and powdery snow was streaming over the ground like smoke. The petallike clouds had completely covered the sun.

"Look," said Renn beside him. She was pointing east.

He glanced around and saw clouds boiling up over the ice cliffs. "Oh no," he murmured.

"Oh yes," said Renn. She had to raise her voice above the wind. "A snowstorm."

The ice river had woken up. And it was angry.

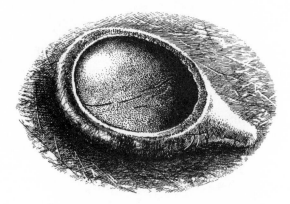

TWENTY-FIVE

The fury of the storm broke upon them with terrifying force.

Torak had to lean into the blast just to stay standing, and clutch his cape to stop it from being ripped away. Through the streaming snow, he saw Renn pushing forward with all her strength; Wolf staggering sideways, his eyes slitted against the wind. The ice river had them in its grip and it wasn't letting go. It howled till Torak's ears ached, and scoured his face with flying ice; it spun him around till he could no longer see Renn, or Wolf, or even his own boots. At any moment it might hurl him into an ice hole. . . .

Through the swirling whiteness, he caught sight of a dark pillar. A rock? A snowdrift? Could it be that they'd finally reached the edge of the ice river?

Renn grabbed his arm. "We can't go on!" she shouted. "We've got to dig in and wait till it's over!"

"Not yet!" he yelled. "Look! We're nearly there!"

He battled on toward the pillar. It shattered and blew apart. It was nothing but a snow cloud: the ice river's vicious trick. He turned to Renn. "You're right! We've got to dig a snow cave!"

But Renn was gone.

"Renn! *Renn!*" The wind tore her name from his lips and whirled it away into the gathering dusk.

He dropped to his knees and groped for Wolf. His mitten found fur, and he clutched the cub. Wolf was casting around for Renn's scent. But what could even a wolf pick up in this?

Amazingly, Wolf pricked his ears and stared straight ahead. Torak thought he saw a figure gliding through the snow. *"Renn!"*

Wolf leaped after it, and Torak followed, but he hadn't gone far when the wind threw him against solid ice. He fell back, nearly crushing the cub. He'd blundered into what looked like an ice hill. In its side was a hole just big enough to crawl through. A snow cave? Surely Renn wouldn't have had time to dig one so quickly?

With one bound, Wolf disappeared inside. After a

moment's hesitation, Torak followed.

The clamor of the storm died down as he crawled into the darkness. With ice-caked mittens he felt out his surroundings. A low roof, so low that he had to crouch on hands and knees; a slab of ice by the entrance hole. Someone must have cut it for a door. But who?

"Renn?" he called.

No reply.

He pushed the slab across the hole, and the stillness closed in around him. He could hear Wolf licking the snow from his paws; ice sliding from his own shoulders.

He put out his hand, and Wolf gave a warning growl.

Torak snatched his hand away. The hairs on the back of his neck began to prickle. Renn wasn't in here—but something was. Something that waited in the dark. "Who's there?" he said.

The icy blackness seemed to tense.

Wrenching off his mittens with his teeth, he whipped out his knife. *"Who's there?"*

Still no answer. He groped for one of Renn's rush-lights. His fingers were so cold that he dropped his tinder pouch. It took forever to find it again; to hit the flint against the strike-fire, and shower sparks on the little pile of yew bark shavings in his hand, but at last the rushlight flared.

He cried out. He forgot about the ice river, he even forgot about Renn.

Almost touching his knee lay a man.

He was dead.

Torak flattened himself against the ice wall. If Wolf hadn't warned him, he would have touched the corpse— and to touch the dead is to risk terrible danger. When the souls leave the body, they can be angry, confused, or simply unwilling to embark on the Death Journey. If one of the living strays too close, the disembodied souls may try to possess it, or follow it home.

All this rushed through Torak's mind as he stared at the dead man.

His lips looked chiseled from ice; his flesh was waxen yellow. Snow had drifted into his nostrils in a cruel parody of breath, but his ice-filmed eyes were open, staring at something Torak couldn't see: something that was cradled in the crook of his dead arm.

Wolf seemed unafraid, even drawn to the corpse. He lay with his muzzle between his paws, gazing at it steadily.

The dead man had worn his long brown hair loose, except for a single lock at the temple, matted with red ochre. Torak thought of the Red Deer woman at Fin-Kedinn's clan meet; she'd worn her hair the same way. Had this man been of the same clan? The same clan as Torak's own mother?

He felt the stirrings of pity. What was the man's

name? What had he been seeking out here, and how had he died?

Then Torak saw that on the brown forehead, a shaky circle had been daubed in red ochre. The thick winter parka had been wrenched open, and another circle drawn on the breastbone. Torak guessed that if he were reckless enough to remove the heavy, furred boots, he'd find a similar mark on each heel. Death Marks. The man must have felt death coming for him, and put on his own marks so that his souls would stay together after he died. That must be why he'd left the slab ajar, too: to set the souls free.

"You were brave," said Torak out loud. "You didn't flinch from death." He remembered the figure he'd glimpsed in the snow. Had that been one of the souls setting out on its final journey? Could you see souls? Torak didn't know.

"Be at peace," he told the corpse. "May your souls find their rest, and stay together." He bowed his head for his dead kinsman.

Wolf sat up, pricking his ears at the corpse. Torak was startled. Wolf seemed to be listening.

Torak leaned closer.

The dead man gazed calmly at the thing cradled in his arm. But when Torak saw what it was, he was even more puzzled. It was an ordinary lamp: a smooth oval of red sandstone about half the size of his palm, with a shallow bowl to hold the fish oil and a groove for the wick of twisted beard-moss. The wick had long since burned away, and all that remained of the oil was a faint grayish stain.

Beside him, Wolf gave a high, soft whine. His hackles were up but he didn't seem frightened. That whine had been—a greeting.

Torak frowned. Wolf had acted like that before. In the cave below the Thunder Falls.

His eyes returned to the dead man. He pictured his final moments: curled in the snow, watching the small, bright flame as his own life flickered and sank . . .

Suddenly, Torak knew. *Coldest of all, the darkest light.* The darkest light is the last light a man sees before he dies.

He had found the third piece of the Nanuak.

Gripping the rushlight in one hand, Torak untied the raven-skin pouch with the other and tipped the box into the snow.

"Uff!" warned Wolf.

Torak slipped off the hair cord and lifted the lid. The river eyes stared blindly up at him, nestled in the curve of the black stone tooth. There was just enough room beside them for the lamp: almost, he thought, as if Renn had known how big to make the box.

With numb fingers he pulled on one mitten and

leaned over the dead man—being careful not to touch him—and lifted the lamp clear. It was only when he'd got it safely boxed and back in the pouch that he realized he'd been holding his breath.

It was time to go and find Renn. Quickly he tied the pouch to his belt. But as he turned to push the slab aside, something made him stop.

He had all three pieces of the Nanuak. Here, in this snow cave, where he was safe.

"If you get caught in a snowstorm," Renn had said, "you dig yourself a snow cave and wait till it stops." If he ignored that now—if he braved the wrath of the ice river to look for her—he probably wouldn't survive. The Nanuak would be buried with him. The entire Forest would be doomed.

If he didn't, Renn might die.

Torak sat back on his heels. Wolf watched him intently, his amber eyes quite un-cublike.

The rushlight wavered in Torak's hand. He couldn't just leave her. She was his friend. But could he—should he—risk the Forest to save her?

As never before, he longed for Fa. Fa would know what to do. . . .

But Fa isn't here, he told himself. *You've* got to decide. You, Torak. By yourself.

Wolf tilted his head to one side, waiting to see what Torak would do.

TWENTY-SIX

"*Torak!*" yelled Renn at the top of her voice. "Torak! Wolf! Where *are* you!"

She was alone in the storm. They could be three paces away and she'd never see them. They could have fallen down an ice hole and she'd never hear the screams.

The wind tossed her into a drift, and she choked on snow. One of her mittens slipped off, and the ice river blew it away. "*No!*" she shouted, beating the snow with her fists. "No, no, no!"

On her hands and knees, she crawled into the wind. Stay calm. Find solid snow. Dig in.

After an endless struggle, she hit a snow hill. The

wind had packed it hard, but not so hard that it was solid ice. Wrenching her axe from her belt, she began hacking a hole.

Torak's probably doing the same thing, she told herself. By the Spirit, I hope so.

With surprising speed, she hacked out a hollow just big enough to take herself and her pack, if she curled up small. The digging warmed her, but she could no longer feel her mittenless hand.

Crawling in backward, she piled the scooped-out chunks in the entrance hole, walling herself up in the freezing darkness. Her breath soon melted the ice that caked her clothes, and she began to shake. As her eyes adjusted to the gloom, she saw that her mittenless fingers were white and hard. She tried to flex them, but they didn't move.

She knew about frostbite: the Boar Clan Leader's son, Aki, had lost three toes to it last winter. If she didn't warm up her fingers soon, they'd turn black and die; then she'd have to cut them off, or she would die too. Desperately, she blew on them, then shoved her hand inside her jerkin, under her armpit. The hand felt heavy and cold, no longer part of her.

Fresh terrors arose. Would she die alone, like her father? Would she never see Fin-Kedinn again? Where were Torak and Wolf? Even if they survived, how would she find them?

Pulling off her remaining mitten, she fumbled at her neck for the grouse-bone whistle that Torak had given her. She blew hard. It made no sound. Was she doing it right? Would Wolf be able to hear it? Maybe it only worked for Torak. Maybe you had to be the Listener.

She blew till she felt giddy and sick. They won't come, she thought. They'll have dug in long ago. If they're still alive.

The whistle tasted salty. Was that the grouse bone, or was she crying? No point crying, she told herself. Screwing her eyes shut, she went on blowing.

She awoke to find herself floating in beautiful heat. The snow was as warm and soft as reindeer skins. She snuggled into it, so drowsy that she couldn't even lift her eyelids . . . much too drowsy to crawl into her sleeping-sack. . . .

Voices dragged her awake. Fin-Kedinn and Saeunn had come to visit her.

I wish they'd let me sleep, she thought hazily.

Her brother was sneering, as he always did. "Why did she make it so small? Why can't she ever do things properly?"

"Hord, that's not true," said Fin-Kedinn. "She did her best."

"Still," said Saeunn, "she could have made a better door."

"I was too tired," mumbled Renn.

Just then, the door blew open, scattering ice all over her. "Shut the door!" she protested.

One of the camp dogs jumped on top of her, showering her with snow, and nudging his cold nose under her chin. She batted him away. "Bad dog! Go *away*!"

"Wake up, Renn!" Torak shouted in her ear.

"I'm *asleep*," murmured Renn, burying her face in the snow.

"No you're not!" shouted Torak. He was longing for sleep himself, but first he had to make room for himself and Wolf, and waken Renn. If she fell asleep now, it would be forever. "Renn, come *on*!" He grabbed her shoulders and shook her. "Wake up!"

"Leave me alone," she said. "I'm fine."

But she wasn't. Her face was blotched and inflamed by the flying ice, her eyes almost swollen shut. The fingers of her right hand were hard and waxy, un-nervingly like those of the Red Deer corpse.

As Torak hacked at the snow, he wondered how much longer she would have lasted if Wolf hadn't found her; and how much longer he and Wolf would have lasted if they hadn't found her snow cave. Torak was nearly worn out; he'd never have had the strength to start one afresh.

Of the three of them, Wolf was holding up the best.

His fur was so thick that the snow lay on top of it without even melting. One good shake and the snow flew off, showering them all.

Swaying with exhaustion, Torak finished enlarging the snow cave and walled up the entrance again, leaving a gap at the top to let out the smoke from the fire he'd promised himself. Then he knelt beside Renn and, after several attempts, dragged her sleeping-sack out from behind her. "Get into this," he growled.

She kicked it away.

Scooping snow between his frozen fists, he rubbed it into her face and hands.

"Ow!" she yelped.

"Wake up or I'll kill you," he snarled.

"You *are* killing me," she snapped.

Knowing he had to make a fire soon, he rubbed his own hands in the snow, then tried to warm them in his armpits. As feeling returned, so did pain. "Ow," he moaned. "Ow, ow, it hurts."

"What did you say?" said Renn, sitting up and banging her head on the ceiling.

"Nothing."

"Yes you did, you were talking to yourself."

"I was talking to myself? You were chatting to your entire clan!"

"I was not," she retorted indignantly.

"You were," he said with a grin. She was waking

up at last. He'd never been so glad to be having an argument.

Somehow, between them, they managed to make a fire. Fire needs warmth as well as air, so they used some of their firewood to make a little platform to keep the rest off the snow—and this time, instead of fumbling with his strike-fire, Torak remembered the fire roll in his pack. At first the fire in the birch-bark roll refused to wake up, even when he blew on it coaxingly and Renn fed it morsels of tinder warmed in her hands. Eventually it flared, rewarding their efforts with a small but cheering blaze.

With dripping hair and chattering teeth, they huddled over it, moaning as it thawed their hands and blistered their faces. But the flames gave them comfort greater than heat. Every night of their lives they'd gone to sleep to that crackling hiss and that bittersweet tang of woodsmoke. The fire was a little piece of the Forest.

Torak found his last roll of dried deer meat and shared it among the three of them. Renn gave him the waterskin. He hadn't known he was thirsty, but as he took a long drink, he felt strength returning.

"How did you find me?" Renn asked.

"I didn't," he replied. "Wolf did. I don't know how."

She considered that. "I think I do." She showed him the grouse-bone whistle.

Torak thought of her blowing that silent whistle in

the dark. He wondered what it had been like, all alone. At least he'd had Wolf.

He told her about the Red Deer corpse, and finding the third part of the Nanuak. He didn't mention the awful moment when he'd considered not trying to find her. He felt too ashamed.

"A stone lamp," murmured Renn. "I wouldn't have thought of that."

"Do you want to see it?"

She shook her head. After a while she said, "If it had been me, I'd have thought twice about leaving the snow cave. You were risking the Nanuak."

Torak was silent. Then he said, "I did think twice. I thought about staying, and not going to look for you."

She went quiet. "Well," she said. "I'd have done the same."

Torak didn't know if he felt better or worse for telling her. "But what would you have *done*?" he asked. "Would you have stayed? Or gone to look for me?"

Renn wiped her nose on the back of her hand. Then she flashed him her sharp-toothed grin. "Who knows? But maybe—it was another kind of test? Not whether you could find the third piece of the Nanuak. But whether you could risk it for a friend."

Torak awoke to a hushed blue glow. He didn't know where he was.

"Storm's over," said Renn. "And I've got a crick in my neck."

So had Torak. Huddled in his sleeping-sack, he turned to face her.

Her eyes were no longer swollen, but her face was red and peeling. When she smiled, it obviously hurt. "Ow!" she croaked. "We survived!"

He grinned back, then wished he hadn't. His face felt as if it had been scrubbed with sand. He probably looked just like Renn. "Now all we've got to do is get off the ice river," he said.

Wolf was whining to be let out. Torak groped for his axe and hacked a hole. Light streamed in, and Wolf shot out. Torak crawled after him.

He emerged into a glittering world of snow hills and wind-carved ridges. The sky was intensely blue, as if it had been washed clean. The stillness was absolute. The ice river had gone back to sleep.

Without warning, Wolf pounced on him, knocking him into a snowdrift. Before he could get up, Wolf leaped onto his chest, grinning and wagging his tail. Laughing, Torak lunged for him, but Wolf dodged out of his reach, then spun around in midair and bowed down with his tail curled over his back. *Let's play!*

Torak went down on his forearms. *Come on then!*

Wolf launched himself at Torak, and together they rolled over and over, Wolf play-biting and tearing at

Torak's hair, and Torak muzzle-grabbing and tugging at his scruff. Finally, Torak tossed a snowball high, and Wolf made one of his amazing twisting leaps and snapped it up, landing in a snowdrift and surfacing with a neat pile of snow on top of his nose.

As Torak struggled breathlessly to his feet, he heard Renn making her way out of the snow cave. "I hope"—she yawned—"it's not too far to the Forest. What happened to your cape?"

He was about to tell her that the storm had ripped it away, when he turned—and forgot about the cape.

East beyond the snow cave—beyond the ice river itself—the High Mountains were terrifyingly close.

For many days the fog had hidden them; then yesterday the ice cliffs had loomed so close that nothing could be seen beyond them. Now, in the clear, cold light, the Mountains ate up the sky.

Torak reeled. For the first time in his life, they weren't just a distant darkness on the eastern horizon. He stood at their very roots: craning his neck at vast, swooping ice faces, at black peaks that pierced the clouds. He felt their power and menace. They were the abode of spirits. Not of men.

Somewhere among them, he thought, lies the Mountain of the World Spirit. *The Mountain I swore to find.*

TWENTY-SEVEN

The red eye was rising. Torak had only a few days to find the Mountain.

Even if he found it, what then? What did he actually have to *do* with the Nanuak? How would he ever destroy the bear?

Renn crunched through the snow to stand beside him. "Come on," she said. "We've got to get off the ice river, back to the Forest."

At that moment, Wolf gave a start and ran to the top of a snow ridge, turning his ears toward the foothills.

"What is it?" whispered Renn. "What's he heard?"

Then Torak heard it too: voices far away in the

Mountains, weaving together in the wild, ever-changing song of the wolf pack.

Wolf flung back his head, pointed his muzzle to the sky, and howled. *I'm here! I'm here!*

Torak was astonished. Why was he howling to a strange pack? Lone wolves didn't do that. They tried to avoid strange wolves.

With a whine, he asked Wolf to come to him—but Wolf stayed where he was: eyes slitted, black lips curled over his teeth as he poured out his song. Torak noticed that he was looking much less puppyish. His legs were longer, and he was growing a mantle of thick black fur around his shoulders. Even his howl was losing its cublike wobble.

"What's he telling them?" asked Renn.

Torak swallowed. "He's telling them where he is."

"And what are they saying?"

Torak listened, never taking his eyes off Wolf. "They're talking to two of their pack: scouts who've gone down onto the fells to seek reindeer. It sounds—" He paused. "Yes, they've found a small herd. The scouts are telling the others where it is, and that they should howl with their muzzles in the snow."

"Why? What for?"

"It's a trick wolves do sometimes, so the reindeer think they're farther away than they really are."

Renn looked uneasy. "You can tell all that?"

He shrugged.

She dug at the snow with her heel. "I don't like it when you talk wolf. It feels strange."

"I don't like it when Wolf talks to other wolves," said Torak. "That feels strange, too."

Renn asked him what he meant, but he didn't reply. It was too painful to put into words. He was beginning to realize that although he knew wolf talk, he was not, and never would be, truly *wolf*. In some ways, he would always be apart from the cub.

Wolf stopped howling and trotted down from the ridge. Torak knelt and put his arm around him. He felt the fine light bones beneath the dense winter fur; the fierce beat of a loyal heart. As he bent to take in the cub's sweet-grass scent, Wolf licked his cheek, then gently pressed his forehead against Torak's own.

Torak shut his eyes tight. *Never leave me*, he wanted to tell Wolf. But he didn't know how to say it.

They started north.

It was an exhausting trudge. The storm had packed the snow into frozen ridges, with thigh-deep troughs in between. Mindful of ice holes, Torak prodded the snow in front of them with his quiver, which slowed them down even more. Always they felt the Mountains watching them, waiting to see if they would fail.

By noon they'd made little progress and were still

within sight of the snow cave. Then they encountered a new obstacle: a wall of ice. It was too steep to climb, and too hard to cut through. Another of the ice river's savage jokes.

Renn said she'd investigate while Torak waited with the cub. He was glad of the rest: The raven-skin pouch was weighing him down. "Watch out for ice holes," he warned, watching anxiously as she peered into a crack between two of the tallest fangs of ice.

"It looks as if there might be a way through," she called. Unslinging her pack, she squeezed in, then disappeared.

Torak was about to go after her when she stuck out her head. "Oh Torak, come and see! We've done it! We've done it!"

Wolf leaped after her. Torak took off his pack and followed them in. He hated edging through the crack—it reminded him of the cave—but when he got to the other side, he gasped.

He was looking down at a torrent of jumbled ice like a frozen waterfall. Below it stretched a long slope of snowy boulders, and beyond that, scarcely a pebble's throw away, and shimmering in its white winter mantle, lay the Forest.

"I never thought I'd see it again," said Renn fervently.

Wolf raised his muzzle to catch the smells, then

glanced back at Torak and wagged his tail.

Torak couldn't speak. He hadn't known how much it had hurt—actually hurt—to be out of the Forest. They'd only spent three nights away, but it felt like moons.

By midafternoon, they'd clambered off the last ice ridge and started zigzagging down the slope. The shadows were turning violet. Pine trees beckoned with snow-heavy boughs. It was a huge relief to get in among them, out of sight of the Mountains. But the stillness was unnerving.

"It can't be the bear," whispered Renn. "There was no sign of it on the ice river. And if it had gone around by the valleys, it would've taken days."

Torak glanced at Wolf. His ears were back, but his hackles were down. "I don't think it's close," he said. "But it isn't far, either."

"Look at this," said Renn, pointing at the snow beneath a juniper tree. "Bird tracks."

Torak stooped to examine them. "A raven. Walking, not hopping. That means it wasn't frightened. And there was a squirrel here too." He pointed to a scattering of cones at the base of a pine tree, each one gnawed to the core like an apple. "And hare tracks. Quite fresh. I can still see some fur marks."

"If they're fresh, that's a good sign," said Renn.

"Mm." Torak peered into the gloom. "But *that* isn't."

The auroch lay on its side like a great brown boulder. In life it had stood taller than the tallest man, and the span of its gleaming black horns had been almost as wide. But the bear had slashed open its belly, leaving it in a churned-up mess of crimson snow.

Torak gazed down at the great ruined beast and felt a surge of anger. Despite their size, aurochs are gentle creatures who use their horns only to fight for mates or defend their young. This blunt-nosed bull had not deserved such a brutal death.

Its carcass hadn't even fed the other creatures of the Forest. No foxes or pine martens had gone near it; no ravens had feasted here. Nothing would touch the prey of the bear.

"Uff," said Wolf, running about in circles with his hackles up.

Stay back, warned Torak. The light was fading, but he could still make out the bear tracks, and he didn't want Wolf touching them.

"It doesn't look like a fresh kill," said Renn. "That's something, isn't it?"

Torak studied the carcass, careful to avoid touching the tracks. He prodded it with a stick, then nodded. "Frozen solid. A day or so at least."

Behind him, Wolf growled.

Torak wondered why he was so agitated when the kill wasn't fresh.

"Somehow," said Renn, "I thought we'd be safer now that we're back in the Forest. I thought—"

But Torak never found out what she thought. Suddenly the snow beneath the trees erupted, and several tall, white-clad figures surrounded them.

Too late, Torak realized that Wolf had not been growling at the auroch—but at these silent assailants. *Look behind you, Torak.* He'd forgotten. Again.

Drawing his knife in one hand and his axe in the other, he edged toward Renn, who already had her knife drawn. Wolf sped into the shadows. Back to back, Torak and Renn faced a bristling circle of arrows.

The tallest of the white-clad figures stepped forward and threw back his hood. In the dusk, his dark-red hair looked almost black. "Got you at last," said Hord.

TWENTY-EIGHT

"**W**hy are you doing this?" cried Renn. "He's trying to help us! You can't treat him like an outcast!"

"Watch me," said Hord, dragging Torak through the snow.

Torak fought to stay on his feet, but it wasn't easy with his hands tied behind his back. There was no hope of escape: he was surrounded by Oslak and four sturdy Raven men.

"Faster!" urged Hord. "We've got to reach camp before dark!"

"But he's the *Listener*!" said Renn. "I can prove it!" She pointed at the raven-skin pouch at Torak's waist.

"He found all three pieces of the Nanuak!"

"Did he," muttered Hord. Without breaking stride, he drew his knife and cut the pouch from Torak's belt. "Well, now they're mine."

"What are you doing?" cried Renn. "Give it back!"

"Hold your tongue!" snapped Hord.

"Why should I? Who says you can—"

Hord slapped her. It was a hard blow across the face, and she went flying, landing in a heap.

Oslak growled a protest, but Hord warned him back. He was breathing hard as he watched Renn sitting up. "You're no longer my sister," he spat. "We thought you were dead when we found your quiver in the stream. Fin-Kedinn didn't speak for three days, but *I* didn't grieve. I was glad. You betrayed your clan, and you shamed me. I wish you *were* dead."

Renn put a trembling hand to her lip. It was bleeding. A red weal was coming up on her cheek.

"You shouldn't have hit her," said Torak.

Hord turned on him. "Keep out of this!"

Torak looked hard at Hord—and was shocked by the change in him. Instead of the stocky young man he'd fought less than a moon ago, he was facing a gaunt shadow. Hord's eyes were raw from sleeplessness, and the hand that clutched the Nanuak had no fingernails, just oozing sores. Something was eating him up from inside.

"Stop staring at me," he snarled.

"Hord," said Oslak, "we've got to keep moving. The bear . . ."

Hord wheeled round, his eyes straining to pierce the darkness. "The bear, the bear," he muttered, as if the very thought hurt.

"Come, Renn." Oslak leaned down and offered his hand. "We'll soon have a poultice on that. Camp's not far."

Renn ignored him and got to her feet unaided.

Glancing up the trail, Torak caught an orange flicker in the deepening dusk. Nearer, in the shadows beneath a young spruce, a pair of amber eyes.

His heart turned over. If Hord saw Wolf, there was no knowing what he might do. . . .

Luckily, Renn had everyone's attention. "Is my brother Clan Leader now?" she demanded. "Do you follow him instead of Fin-Kedinn?"

The men hung their heads.

"It's not that simple," said Oslak. "The bear attacked three days ago. It killed—" His voice cracked. "It killed two of us."

The blood drained from Renn's face. She drew closer to Oslak, whose brow and cheekbones were marked with gray river clay.

Torak didn't know what the marks meant, but when Renn saw them she gasped. "No," she whispered, touching Oslak's hand.

The big man nodded and turned away.

"What about Fin-Kedinn?" Renn said shrilly. "Is he—"

"Badly wounded," said Hord. "If he dies, I *will* be Leader. I'll make sure of it."

Renn clapped her hands to her mouth and raced off toward the camp.

"Renn!" shouted Oslak. "Come back!"

"Let her go," said Hord.

When she'd gone, Torak felt utterly alone. He didn't even know the names of the other Raven men. "Oslak," he begged, "make Hord give me back the Nanuak! It's our only hope. You know that."

Oslak started to speak, but Hord cut in. "Your part in this is finished," he told Torak. "*I* will take the Nanuak to the Mountain! *I* will offer the blood of the Listener to save my people!"

Wolf was so frightened that he wanted to howl. How could he help his pack-brother? Why was everything so chewed up?

As he followed the full-grown taillesses through the Bright Soft Cold, he struggled against the hunger gnawing his belly, and the muzzle-watering smell of the lemmings just a pounce away. He fought against the Pull that was now so strong that he felt it all the time, and the fear of the demon he scented on the wind. He turned his ears from the distant howls of the stranger pack: the pack that didn't sound like strangers anymore, but faraway kin . . .

He had to ignore it all. His pack-brother was in danger. Wolf sensed his pain and fear. He sensed, too, the anger of the full-growns, and *their* fear. They were scared of Tall Tailless.

The wind changed, and Wolf caught a wave of scents from the great Den of the taillesses. Sounds and smells overwhelmed him. *Bad, bad, bad!* His courage failed. Whimpering, he shot under a fallen tree.

The Den meant terrible danger. It was huge and complicated, with angry dogs who didn't listen, and many of the Bright Beasts-That-Bite-Hot. Worst of all were the taillesses themselves. They couldn't hear or smell much, but they made up for it by doing clever things with their forepaws and sending the Long-Claw-That-Flies to bite the prey.

Wolf didn't know whether to run or stay.

To help himself think, he chewed a branch, then a chunk of the Bright Soft Cold. He ran in circles. Nothing worked. He longed for the strange sureness that sometimes came to him and told him what to do. It didn't come. It had flown like a raven into the Up.

What must he *do*?

Torak blamed himself. Because of his carelessness, he'd lost the Nanuak. It was all his fault. Around him the snow-laden trees cast blue moon shadows across the trail. "Your fault," they seemed to be telling him.

"Faster," said Hord, jabbing him in the back.

The Ravens had camped in a clearing by a mountain stream. At the heart of the clearing, a long-fire of three pine logs glowed orange. Clustered around it were the clan's sloping shelters, then a ring of smaller fires and spiked pits, guarded by men with spears. It looked as if the entire clan had come north.

Hord ran ahead while Torak waited with Oslak by one of the shelters. He saw Renn, and his spirits rose. She was kneeling at the mouth of a shelter on the other side of the clearing, talking urgently. She didn't see him.

People were huddled around the long-fire. The air was thick with fear. According to Oslak, scouts had found signs of the bear only two valleys away. "It's getting stronger," he said. "Tearing up the Forest as if—as if it's seeking something."

Torak started to shiver. Hord's forced march had kept him warm, but now, in his summer buckskin, he was freezing. He hoped they wouldn't think he was scared.

Oslak untied his wrists and put his hand on his shoulder to guide him into the clearing. Torak forgot about the cold as he stumbled into the glare of the long-fire, and a buzz of voices like a hive of angry bees.

He saw Saeunn, cross-legged on a pile of reindeer hides with the raven-skin pouch in her lap; Hord beside her, gnawing his thumb; Dyrati watching Hord, her face strained.

Silence fell. People made way for four men bearing Fin-Kedinn on an auroch-hide litter. The Raven Leader's face was drawn, and his left leg was bandaged in soft bindings blotched with blood. His face contracted slightly as the men set him down by the long-fire. It was the only sign he gave of being in pain.

Renn appeared, rolling a chunk of pine log. She put it behind Fin-Kedinn for him to lean against, then curled up beside him on a reindeer skin. She didn't look at Torak but kept her eyes on the fire.

Oslak nudged him in the back, and he took a few halting steps closer to the litter.

The Raven Leader caught his gaze and held it, and Torak felt a rush of relief. The blue eyes were as intense and unreadable as ever. Hord would have to wait a while longer to be Clan Leader.

"When we first found this boy," said Fin-Kedinn, his voice ringing clear, "we didn't know who, or what, he was. Since then, he has found the three pieces of the Nanuak. He has saved the life of one of our own." He paused. "I have no more doubts. He is the Listener. The question is, do we let him take the Nanuak to the

Mountain? A boy, on his own? Or do we send our strongest hunter: a full-grown man with a far greater chance against the bear?"

Hord stopped gnawing his thumb and squared his shoulders. Torak's heart sank.

"Time is short," said Fin-Kedinn, glancing at the night sky where the Great Auroch blazed. "In a few days, the bear will be too strong to overcome. We can't call a clan meet; there's no time. I must decide this now, for all the clans."

The only sound was the hiss and crackle of the fire. The Ravens were hanging on every word.

"There are many among us," Fin-Kedinn went on, "who say it would be madness to trust our fate to a boy."

Hord leaped to his feet. "It *would* be madness! *I'm* the strongest! Let me go to the Mountain and save my people!"

"You're not the Listener," said Torak.

"What about the rest of the Prophecy?" said Saeunn in her raven's croak. "'*The Listener gives his heart's blood to the Mountain.*' Could you do that?"

Torak took a breath. "If that's what it takes."

"But there's another way!" cried Hord. "We kill him now, and I take his blood to the Mountain! At least then we stand a chance!"

A murmur of approval from the Ravens.

Fin-Kedinn raised a hand for silence, then spoke to Torak. "You used to deny that you were the Listener. Why so eager now?"

Torak raised his chin. "The bear killed my father. That's what it was made to do."

"This is greater than vengeance!" sneered Hord.

"It's greater than vanity, too," Torak retorted. He spoke to Fin-Kedinn. "I don't care about being 'the savior of my people.' What people? I've never even met my own clan. But I swore to my father that I'd find the Mountain. I swore an oath."

"We're wasting time!" said Hord. "Give me the Nanuak and I will do it!"

"How?" said a quiet voice.

It was Renn.

"How will you find the Mountain?" she asked.

Hord hesitated.

Renn stood up. "It's said to be the farthest peak at the northernmost end of the High Mountains. Well, here we are, at the northernmost end of the High Mountains. So where is it?" She spread her hands. "I don't know." She turned to Hord. "Do you?"

He ground his teeth.

She spoke to Saeunn. "Do you? No. And you're the Mage." She faced Fin-Kedinn. "Do you?"

"No," he answered.

Renn pointed at Torak. "Not even he knows where

it is, and he's the Listener." She paused. "But some-body knows." She looked directly at Torak, her eyes drilling into his.

He caught her meaning. Clever Renn, he thought. Just so long as it works . . .

He put his hands to his lips and howled.

The Ravens gasped. The camp dogs leaped into uproar.

Again Torak howled.

Suddenly, a streak of gray sped across the clearing and crashed into him.

People muttered and pointed; the dogs went wild until men shooed them away. A small child laughed.

Torak knelt and buried his face in Wolf's fur. Then he gave the cub's muzzle a grateful lick. It had taken enormous courage for Wolf to answer his call.

As the uproar subsided, Torak raised his head. "Only Wolf can find the Mountain," he told Fin-Kedinn. "He got us this far. It's only because of him that we found the Nanuak."

The Raven Leader ran a hand over his dark-red beard.

"Give me back the Nanuak," pleaded Torak. "Let me take it to the World Spirit. It's our only chance."

The fire crackled and spat. Snow thudded off a nearby spruce. The Ravens waited for their Leader's decision.

At last Fin-Kedinn spoke. "We'll give you food and clothing for the journey. When do you leave?"

Hord shouted a protest, but Fin-Kedinn silenced him with a glance. Again he spoke to Torak. "When do you leave?"

Torak swallowed. "Um. Tomorrow?"

TWENTY-NINE

Tomorrow, Torak and Wolf would set out into the bear-haunted Forest—and Torak had no idea what he was going to do.

Even if they reached the Mountain, what next? Should he simply leave the Nanuak on the ground? Ask the World Spirit to destroy the bear? Try to fight it on his own?

"Do you want new boots, or do we mend yours?" snapped Oslak's mate, who was measuring him for winter clothes.

"What?" he said.

"Boots," repeated the woman. She had tired eyes

and river clay markings on her cheeks—and she was furious with him. He didn't know why.

He said, "I'm used to my boots. Could you maybe—"

"Mend them?" She snorted. "I think I can manage that!"

"Thank you," Torak said humbly. He glanced at Wolf, who was cowering in the corner with his ears back.

Oslak's mate snatched a length of sinew and spun Torak around to measure his shoulders. "Oh, it'll fit all right," she muttered. "Well, sit down, sit down!"

Torak sat, and watched her tying knots to mark the measurements. Her eyes were moist, and she was blinking rapidly. She caught him looking. "What are you staring at?"

"Nothing," he replied. "Should I take off my clothes?"

"Not unless you want to freeze. You'll have the new things by dawn. Now give me the boots."

He did, and she eyed them as if they were a pair of rotting salmon. "More holes than a fishing net," she said. It was a relief when she bustled out of the shelter.

She hadn't been gone long when Renn came in. Wolf padded over and licked her fingers. She scratched him behind the ears.

Torak wanted to thank her for standing up for him, but he wasn't sure how to start. The silence lengthened.

"How'd you get on with Vedna?" Renn said abruptly.

"Vedna? Oh. Oslak's mate? I don't think she likes me."

"It's not that. It's your new clothes. She was making them for her son. Now she's got to finish them for you."

"Her son?"

"Killed by the bear."

"Oh." Poor Vedna, he thought. Poor Oslak. And that explained the river clay. It must be the Raven way of mourning.

The bruise on Renn's cheek had turned purple; he asked if it hurt. She shook her head. He guessed that she was ashamed of what her brother had done.

"What about Fin-Kedinn?" he said. "How bad is his leg?"

"Bad. Bone-deep. But no sign of the blackening sickness."

"That's good." He hesitated. "Was he—very angry with you?"

"Yes. But that's not why I'm here."

"So why are you here?"

"Tomorrow. I'm coming with you."

Torak bit his lip. "I think it has to be just me and Wolf."

She glared at him. "Why?"

"I don't know. I just do."

"That's stupid."

"Maybe. But that's how it is."

"You sound like Fin-Kedinn."

"That's another reason. He'd never allow it."

"Since when did I let that stop me?"

He grinned.

She didn't grin back. Looking thunderous, she moved to the fire at the entrance to the shelter. "You're to eat nightmeal with him," she said. "It's an honor. In case you didn't know."

Torak swallowed. He was scared of Fin-Kedinn, but in a strange way, he also wanted his approval. Eating nightmeal with him sounded unnerving. "Will you be there too?" he asked.

"No."

"Oh."

Another silence. Then she relented. "If you like, I'll keep Wolf with me. Best not to leave him alone with the dogs."

"Thanks."

She nodded. Then she saw his bare feet. "I'll see if I can find you a pair of boots."

Some time later, Torak made his way to Fin-Kedinn's shelter, stumbling in his borrowed boots, which were much too big.

He found the Raven Leader in heated talk with

Saeunn, but they stopped when he came in. Saeunn looked fierce. Fin-Kedinn's face gave nothing away.

Torak sat cross-legged on a reindeer skin. He couldn't see any food, but people were busy at cooking skins by the long-fire. He wondered how soon they would eat. And what he was doing here.

"I've told you what I think," said Saeunn.

"So you have," Fin-Kedinn said evenly.

They made no attempt to include Torak, which left him free to study Fin-Kedinn's shelter. It was no grander than the others, and from the roof post hung the usual hunter's gear; but the string of the great yew bow was broken, and the white reindeer-hide parka was spattered with dried blood: stark reminders that the Raven Leader had faced the bear and survived.

Suddenly, Torak noticed a man watching him from the shadows. He had short, brown hair and dark, wizened features.

"This is Krukoslik," said Fin-Kedinn, "of the Mountain Hare Clan."

The man put both fists over his heart and bowed his head.

Torak did the same.

"Krukoslik knows these parts better than anyone," said Fin-Kedinn. "Talk to him before you set out. If nothing else, he'll give you a few hints on surviving the Mountains. I wasn't impressed by the state you were in when we caught you. No winter clothes, one waterskin, and no food. Your father taught you better than that."

Torak caught his breath. "So you did know him?"

Saeunn bristled, but Fin-Kedinn quelled her with a glance. "Yes," he said. "I knew him. There was a time when he was my best friend."

Angrily, Saeunn turned away.

Torak felt himself getting angry too. "If you were his best friend, why did you sentence me to death? Why did you let me fight Hord? Why did you keep me tied up while the clan meet decided whether to sacrifice me?"

"To see what you were made of," Fin-Kedinn said calmly. "You're no good to anyone if you can't use your wits." He paused. "If you remember, I didn't keep you under close guard. I even let you have the wolf cub with you."

Torak thought about that. "You mean—you were testing me?"

Fin-Kedinn did not reply.

Two men came over from the main fire, carrying four steaming birchwood bowls.

"Eat," said Krukoslik, handing one to Torak.

Fin-Kedinn tossed over a horn spoon, and for a while Torak forgot about everything as he dug in hungrily. It was a thin broth made from boiled elk hooves and a few slivers of dried deer heart, bulked up with rowanberries and the tough, tasteless tree mushroom that the clans call auroch's ears. With it, they had a single flat cake of roasted acorn meal: very bitter, but not too bad once it was broken up and mashed into the broth.

"I'm sorry we can't do better," said Fin-Kedinn, "but prey is scarce." It was the only reference he made to the bear.

Torak was too hungry to care. Only when he'd licked his bowl did he notice that Fin-Kedinn and Saeunn had hardly touched theirs. Saeunn took them back to the cooking skin, then returned to her place. Krukoslik hung his spoon on his belt and went to kneel by the small fire at the entrance to the shelter, where he murmured a brief prayer of thanks.

Torak had never seen anyone like him. He wore a bulky robe of brown reindeer hide that hung all the way to his calves, and a broad belt of red buckskin. His clan skin was a mantle of hare fur over the shoulders, dyed a fiery red, and his clan-tattoo was a red zigzag band across the forehead. On his breast hung a finger-long shard of smoky rock crystal.

He saw Torak looking at it and smiled. "Smoke is the breath of the Fire Spirit. Mountain clans worship fire above all else."

Torak remembered the comfort the fire had given

him and Renn in the snow cave. "I can understand that," he said.

Krukoslik's smile broadened.

With nightmeal over, Fin-Kedinn asked the others to leave so that he could speak to Torak alone. Krukoslik stood up and bowed. Saeunn gave an angry hiss and swept from the shelter.

Torak wondered what was coming next.

"Saeunn," said Fin-Kedinn, "doesn't think you should be told any more. She thinks it would distract you tomorrow."

"Any more about what?" asked Torak.

"About what you want to know."

Torak considered that. "I want to know everything."

"Not possible. Try again."

Torak picked at a tear in the knee of his leggings. "Why me? Why am I the Listener?"

Fin-Kedinn stroked his beard. "That is a long story."

"Is it because of my father? Because he was the Wolf Mage? The enemy of the crippled wanderer who made the bear?"

"That is—part of it."

"But who was he? Why were they enemies? Fa never even mentioned him."

With a stick, the Raven Leader stirred the fire,

and Torak saw the lines of pain deepen on either side of his mouth. Without turning his head, Fin-Kedinn said, "Did your father ever mention the Soul-Eaters?"

Torak was puzzled. "No. I've never heard of them."

"Then you must be the only one in the Forest who hasn't." Fin-Kedinn fell silent, the firelight etching his face with shadow. "The Soul-Eaters," he went on, "were seven Mages, each from a different clan. In the beginning, they were not evil. They helped their clans. Each had a particular skill. One was subtle as a snake, always delving into the lore of herbs and potions. One was strong as an oak; he wished to know the minds of trees. Another had thoughts that flew swifter than a bat. She loved to enchant small creatures to do her bidding. One was proud and far seeking, fascinated by demons, always trying to control them. They say that another could summon the Dead." Again he stirred the fire.

When he did not continue, Torak mustered his courage. "That's only five. You said—there were seven."

Fin-Kedinn ignored him. "Many winters ago, they banded together in secret. At first they called themselves the Healers. Deceived themselves into believing that they wished only to do good: to cure sickness, guard against demons." His mouth twisted in scorn.

"Soon they drifted into evil, warped by their hunger for power."

Torak's fingers tightened on his knee. "Why were they called Soul-Eaters?" he asked, scarcely moving his lips. "Did they really eat souls?"

"Who knows? People were frightened, and when people are frightened, rumor becomes truth." His face became distant as he remembered. "Above all things, the Soul-Eaters wanted power. That's what they lived for. To rule the Forest. To force everyone in it to do their bidding. Then, thirteen winters ago, something happened that shattered their power."

"What?" whispered Torak. "What happened?"

Fin-Kedinn sighed. "All you need to know is that there was a great fire, and the Soul-Eaters were scattered. Some were badly wounded. All went into hiding. We thought the threat had gone forever. We were wrong." He snapped the stick in two and threw it on the fire. "The man you call the crippled wanderer—the man who created the bear—he was one of them."

"A *Soul-Eater?*"

"I knew as soon as Hord told me about him. Only a Soul-Eater could have trapped so great a demon." He met Torak's eyes. "Your father was his enemy. He was the sworn enemy of all the Soul-Eaters."

Torak couldn't look away from the intense blue

gaze. "He never told me anything."

"He had reasons. Your father—" he said. "Your father did many wrong things in his life. But he did all he could to stop the Soul-Eaters. That's why they killed him. It's also why he brought you up apart. So that they'd never know you even existed."

Torak stared at him. "*Me?* Why?"

Fin-Kedinn wasn't listening. Once again, he was watching the flames. "It doesn't seem possible," he murmured. "Nobody ever suspected there was a son. Not even me."

"But—Saeunn knew. Fa told her, five summers ago at the clan meet by the Sea. Didn't she—"

"No," said Fin-Kedinn. "She never told me."

"I don't understand," said Torak. "Why couldn't the Soul-Eaters know about me? What's wrong with me?"

Fin-Kedinn studied his face. "Nothing. They mustn't know about you because . . ." He shook his head, as if there was too much to tell. "Because one day you might be able to stop them."

Torak was aghast. "*Me?* How?"

"I don't know. I only know that if they find out about you, they'll come after you." Once more his eyes held Torak's. "This is what Saeunn didn't want you to know. And it's what I believe you *must* know. If you live—if you succeed in destroying the bear—it won't be the end. The Soul-Eaters will find out who did it.

They'll know you exist. Sooner or later, they'll come after you."

An ember cracked.

Torak jumped. "You mean—even if I survive tomorrow, I'll be running all my life."

"I didn't say that. You can run or you can fight. There's always a choice."

Torak looked up at the blood-spattered parka. Hord was right: This was a fight for men, not for boys. "Why did Fa never tell me anything?"

"Your father knew what he was doing," said Fin-Kedinn. "He did some bad things. Some things for which I'll never forgive him. But with you, I think he did the right thing."

Torak couldn't speak.

"Ask yourself this, Torak: Why does the Prophecy speak of the Listener? Why not 'the Talker' or 'the Seer'?"

Torak shook his head.

"Because the most important quality in a hunter is to *be* a listener. To listen to what the wind and the trees are telling you. To listen to what other hunters and prey are saying about the Forest. That's the gift your father gave you. He didn't teach you Magecraft, or the story of the clans. He taught you to hunt. To use your wits." He paused. "If you are to succeed tomorrow, that's how you'll do it. By using your wits."

It was after middle-night, but still Torak sat by the long-fire in the clearing, staring at the looming blackness of the High Mountains.

He was alone. Wolf had gone off on his nightly wanderings, and the only signs of life in the camp were the silent Ravens guarding the defenses and the rumble of snores from Oslak's shelter.

Torak longed to find Renn and tell her everything. But he didn't know where she was sleeping. Besides, he wasn't sure that he could bring himself to tell her about Fa—about the bad things Fin-Kedinn said he had done.

"If you live . . . it won't be the end. . . . The Soul-Eaters will come after you. . . . You can run or you can fight. There's always a choice. . . ."

Terrible images whirled in his head like a snowstorm. The bear's murderous eyes. The Soul-Eaters, like half-glimpsed shadows in a bad dream. Fa's face as he lay dying.

To chase them away, he stood up and began to pace. He forced himself to think.

He had no idea what he was going to do tomorrow, but he knew that Fin-Kedinn was right. If he was to stand a chance against the bear, it would be by using his wits. The World Spirit would help him only if he tried to help himself.

Once again, he ran through the lines of the Prophecy. *The Listener fights with air, and speaks with silence. . . . The Listener fights with air. . . .*

The glimmerings of an idea began to nag at him.

THIRTY

Torak's fingers were shaking so much that he couldn't get the stopper off his medicine horn.

Why had he left this to the last moment? Now Wolf was padding restlessly up and down outside the shelter, and the Ravens were waiting to see him off, and he still couldn't get the stopper off the—

"Want some help?" said Renn from the doorway. Her face was pale, her eyes shadowed.

Torak passed her the medicine horn, and she yanked out the black oak stopper with her teeth. "What's this for?" she asked, handing it back.

"Death Marks," he said, not looking at her.

She gasped. "Like the man on the ice river?"

He nodded.

"But he knew he was going to die. You might survive—"

"You don't know that. I don't want to risk my souls getting separated. I don't want to risk becoming a demon."

She stooped to stroke Wolf's ears. "You're right."

Torak glanced past her into the clearing, where the dark-blue dawn was breaking. During the night, clouds had rolled down from the Mountains, covering the Forest in thick snow. He wondered if that would help or hinder him.

He tipped some red ochre onto his palm and spat on it. But his mouth was too dry, and he couldn't make a paste.

Renn leaned over and spat into his palm. Then she scooped up some snow, warmed it in her hands, and added that.

"Thanks," he muttered. Shakily, he daubed circles on his heels, breastbone, and forehead. As he finished the one on his forehead, he shut his eyes. The last time he'd done this had been for Fa.

Wolf pressed against him, rubbing his scent into the new leggings. He put his paw on Torak's forearm. *I'm with you.*

Torak bent and nosed his muzzle. *I know.*

"Here," said Renn, holding out the raven-skin pouch. "I added more wormwood, and I checked with Saeunn. The masking charm should work. The bear won't sense the Nanuak."

Torak tied the pouch to his belt. Already, he could feel the Death Marks stiffening on his skin.

"You'd better take this, too." Renn was holding out a little bundle wrapped in birch bast.

"What is it?"

She looked startled. "What you asked for. What I sat up most of the night making."

He was appalled. He'd almost forgotten. If he'd left without it, what would have become of his plan?

"I've put in some purifying herbs as well," said Renn.

"Why?"

"Well. If—if you kill the bear, you'll be unclean. I mean, it's still a bear, still another hunter, even if there is a demon inside. You'll need to purify yourself."

How like Renn to think ahead. How reassuring that she thought he had a chance.

Wolf gave an impatient whine, and Torak took a deep breath. Time to go.

As they started across the clearing, Torak remembered the medicine horn left behind in the shelter, and ran back for it. As he came out, opening his medicine pouch with trembling fingers, the horn slipped from his grasp.

It was Fin-Kedinn who picked it up.

The Raven Leader was on crutches. As he studied the medicine horn in his hand, the blood drained from his face. "This was your mother's," he said.

Torak blinked. "How did you know?"

Fin-Kedinn was silent. He handed it back. "Don't ever lose it."

Torak stowed the horn in his pouch. That seemed an odd thing to say, given where he was headed. As he was turning to go, Fin-Kedinn called him back. "Torak—"

"Yes?"

"If you survive, there's a place for you here with us. If you want it."

Torak was too surprised to speak. By the time he'd recovered, the Raven Leader was moving away, his face as unyielding as ever.

The High Mountains were rimmed with gold as Torak crunched through the snow toward the Ravens. Oslak handed him his sleeping-sack and waterskin, Renn his axe, quiver, and bow. Surprisingly, Hord helped him on with his pack. He looked haggard but seemed to have accepted that he wasn't the one who would be seeking the Mountain.

Saeunn made the sign of the hand over Torak, and then over Wolf. "May the guardian fly with you both."

"And run with you too," said Renn, trying to smile.

Torak gave her a brief nod. He just wanted to be gone.

The Ravens watched in silence as he started through the snow, with Wolf trotting in his tracks.

He did not look back.

The Forest was hushed, but as Wolf took the lead, he seemed eager and unafraid. Torak plodded behind him, his breath steaming. It was very cold, but thanks to Vedna, he didn't feel it. While he was sleeping, she'd left the new things in his shelter. An underjerkin of duck skin with the breast feathers soft against the skin; a hooded parka and leggings of warm winter reindeer hide; hare fur mittens on a thong threaded through the sleeves; and his old boots, deftly patched with tough reindeer-shin hide, with bands of dogfish skin sewn to the outer soles to improve the grip, and lined with pine marten fur.

Vedna had even unpicked his clan skin from his old jerkin and sewn it to the parka. The band of wolf fur was tattered and filthy but very precious. It had been prepared by Fa.

Wolf swerved to investigate something, and Torak was instantly alert. A squirrel's tracks: tiny and hand-like. Torak followed the trail as it hopped along between snow-covered juniper bushes, then broke into long, startled leaps and disappeared up a pine tree.

Torak threw back his hood and stared about him.

The Forest was utterly still. Whatever had frightened the squirrel had gone. But Torak was angry with himself. He should have spotted those tracks too. Stay alert.

A jay followed them from tree to tree as they pushed on. The sun rose in a cloudless sky. Soon Torak was panting as he labored knee-deep in dazzling new snow. He'd decided against snowshoes: They'd make walking easier but slow him down if he had to move fast.

Wolf fared better, as his narrow chest cut the snow like a canoe slicing water. By midmorning, though, even he was tiring. The land was climbing steadily, as Krukoslik had said it would.

"My grandfather once got close to the Mountain," he'd explained to Torak. "So close that he could feel it. From here, you follow the stream north, and the land climbs till you're in the shadow of the High Mountains. Around midday, you reach a lightning-struck spruce at the mouth of a ravine. The ravine is steep: too steep to climb. But there's a trail that clings to its western side—"

"What kind of trail?" Torak had asked. "Who made it?"

"Nobody knows. Just take it. That lightning tree— it has power to protect. It guards the trail from evil. Maybe it will protect you, too."

"What then? Where do I go then?"

Krukoslik had spread his hands. "You follow the trail. Somewhere, at the end of the ravine, lies the Mountain."

"How far?"

"Nobody knows. My grandfather didn't get far before the Spirit stopped him. The Spirit always stops them. Maybe—maybe you will be different."

Maybe, thought Torak, trudging through the snow.

If his plan worked—if the World Spirit answered his plea—the bear would be destroyed and the Forest would survive. If not, there would be no second chances. For him or the Forest.

In front of him, Wolf raised his head and sniffed. His hackles were up. What had he sensed?

A few paces on, Torak noticed that the snow had been brushed off the tips of the branches at about shoulder height. Then he found a juniper sapling with several twigs raggedly bitten off. "Red deer," he murmured.

A jumble of tracks confirmed it. By the look of them, it was a single deer, probably a buck: they didn't pick up their feet as high as hinds did, and Torak saw drag marks in the snow.

But if it was only a deer, why were Wolf's hackles up?

Torak looked around. He could feel the Forest holding its breath.

The bear tracks leaped out at him from the snow.

He hadn't seen them before because they were so widely spaced, but now he made out the signs of the buck's panicky leap down the slope below, with the bear tracks racing after it. The length of stride was horrifying.

Struggling for calm, Torak forced himself to study the trail. The bear had been going at a gallop, as the pattern of prints was reversed, with the man-shaped hind tracks in front of the broader front tracks. Each one was three times the size of his own head.

They're fresh, he thought, but the edges are slightly rounding over. Although in this sun that wouldn't take long. . . .

Wolf jumped over the tracks, eager to press on.

Torak followed more slowly. Every bush and boulder took on bear form.

As they toiled up the slope, Wolf became more and more excited: bounding ahead, then doubling back for Torak and urging him on with little grunt-whines. Perhaps at last they were nearing the Mountain. Perhaps that was why Wolf was excited rather than frightened. Torak wished he could share that excitement, but all he could feel was the weight of the Nanuak at his belt, and the menace of the bear.

A distant roar split the Forest.

The jay gave a squawk and flew away.

Torak gripped the hilt of his knife so hard that it hurt. How close? Where was it? He couldn't tell.

Wolf was waiting for him to catch up—hackles raised, but tail held high. His meaning was clear: *Not yet.*

As Torak waded through the snow, he wondered what had happened to the bear's own souls. After all, as Renn had said, it was still a bear; once it must have hunted salmon and browsed on berries and slumbered through the winter. Were its souls still inside its body, with the demon? Trapped, terrified?

He rounded a boulder—and there was the lightning-struck spruce.

His spirits quailed.

Above him, the High Mountains swept skyward, blindingly white. The ravine cut through them like a knife slash. On and on it wound into the Mountains, its end lost in impenetrable cloud. A narrow trail clung to its western side, snaking up from where Torak stood. Who had made the trail? For what purpose? Who would dare set foot on it and venture into that haunted place?

Suddenly, the clouds at the end of the ravine parted, and Torak saw what lay beyond. Storm clouds writhed about its flanks; a deep, windless cold flowed from its summit; unimaginably high, it pierced the sky: the Mountain of the World Spirit.

Torak shut his eyes, but he could still feel the power

of the Spirit forcing him to his knees. He could feel its anger. The Soul-Eaters had conjured a demon from the Otherworld; they had loosed a monster on the Forest. They had broken the pact. Why should the Spirit help the clans, when some among them had been so wicked?

Torak bowed his head. He couldn't go on. He didn't belong here. This was the haunt of spirits, not of men.

When he opened his eyes, the Mountain was gone, once more shrouded in clouds.

Torak sat back on his heels. I can't do it, he thought. I can't go up there.

Wolf sat in front of him, his tear-shaped eyes as pure as water. *Yes you can. I'm with you.*

Torak shook his head.

Wolf gazed steadily back at him.

Torak thought of Renn and Fin-Kedinn and the Ravens, and of all the other clans that he didn't even know about. He thought of the countless lives in the Forest. He thought of Fa: not Fa as he lay dying in the wreck of their shelter, but Fa as he'd been just before the bear attacked: laughing at the joke Torak had made.

Grief rose in his chest. He drew his knife from its sheath and slipped off his mitten to lay his hand on the cold blue slate. "You can't stop now," he said out loud. "You swore an oath. To Fa."

He unslung his quiver and bow and laid them against the tree. Then he did the same with his pack, his sleeping-sack, waterskin, and axe. He wouldn't need them; just his knife, the Nanuak in the raven-skin pouch, and Renn's little birch-bast bundle in his medicine pouch.

With a last glance at the Forest, he followed Wolf up the trail.

THIRTY-ONE

A s soon as Torak set foot on the trail, the cold grew
intense. The breath crackled in his nostrils. His eye-
lashes stuck together. The Spirit was warning him back.

The ice under his boots was brittle, and each step
rang out across the ravine. Wolf's soft paws made no
sound. He turned and waited for Torak to catch up: his
muzzle relaxed, his tail wagging faintly. It was as if he
was glad to be here.

Panting, Torak drew level with him. The trail was so
narrow that they only just had room to stand side by
side. Torak glanced down—and wished he hadn't.
Already, the bottom of the ravine was far below.

They climbed higher. The sun cleared the other side of the ravine, and the glare became blinding. The ice turned treacherous. When Torak stepped too close to the edge of the trail, the ice crumbled, and he nearly went over.

About forty paces ahead, the trail widened slightly beneath a rocky overhang. It was too shallow to make a cave: merely a hollow where the black basalt of the ravine's side showed through. At the sight of it, Torak's spirits lifted. He'd been hoping for some kind of shelter. He would need it if his plan—

Beside him, Wolf tensed.

He was looking down into the ravine, his ears forward, every hair on his back standing up.

Shading his eyes, Torak peered over the edge. Nothing. Black tree trunks. Snow-covered boulders. Puzzled, he turned to go—and the bear appeared suddenly, as bears do. First a movement at the bottom of the ravine—then there it was.

Even from this distance—fifty, sixty paces below him—it was enormous. As Torak stood rooted to the spot, it swayed from side to side, casting for a scent.

It didn't find one. Torak was too high up. The bear didn't know he was here. He watched it turn and move off down the ravine, toward the Forest.

Now he had to do the unthinkable. He had to lure it back.

There was only one sure way of doing that. He slipped off his mittens and blew on his fingers to warm them; then he unfastened the raven-skin pouch from his belt. Untying the hair cord that bound it, he opened the rowan-bark box, and the Nanuak stared up at him. The river eyes, the stone tooth, the lamp.

Wolf gave a low grunt-whine.

Torak licked his cold-cracked lips. From his medicine pouch, he took Renn's little birch-bast bundle. He stuffed the purifying herbs and birch-bast wrapping into the neck of his parka, and looked down at what Renn had made for him in the night. A small pouch of knotted woven grass, the mesh so fine that it would hold even the river eyes but let the light of the Nanuak shine out; the light that Torak couldn't see, but the bear could.

Taking care not to touch the Nanuak with his bare hands, he tipped the lamp, the stone tooth, and the river eyes into the woven-grass pouch. Then he drew it shut and looped its long drawstring over his head. He was wearing the Nanuak unmasked on his chest.

Wolf's eyes threw back a faint, shimmering gold light: the light of the Nanuak. If Wolf could see it, so could the demon. Torak was counting on it.

He turned to face the bear. It was some distance down the ravine, moving effortlessly through the snow.

"Here it is," said Torak, keeping his voice low so as

not to anger the World Spirit. "This is what you're after: the brightest of those bright souls that you hate so much—that you long to snuff out forever. Come for it now."

The bear halted. A ripple ran through its massive shoulder hump. The great head swung around. The bear turned and began moving toward Torak.

A fierce exultation surged through him. This monster had killed Fa. Ever since then, he'd been on the run. Now he wasn't running anymore. He was fighting back.

It was faster than Torak expected; soon it was beneath him. Man fashion, it rose on its hind legs. Although Torak stood fifty paces above, he saw it as clearly as if he could reach out and touch it.

It raised its head and met his eyes—and he forgot about the Spirit, he forgot about his oath to Fa. He was not standing on an icy mountain trail, he was back in the Forest. From the ruined shelter came Fa's wild cry. *Torak! Run!*

He couldn't move. He wanted to run—to race up the trail to the overhang, as he knew he must—but he could not. The demon was draining his will—pulling him down, down. . . .

Wolf snarled.

Torak tore himself free and staggered up the trail. Staring into those eyes had been like staring at the sun:

their green-edged image stayed stamped on his mind.

He heard the cracking of ice as the bear began to claw its way up the side of the ravine. He pictured it climbing with lethal ease. He had to reach the overhang, or he wouldn't stand a chance.

Wolf loped up the trail. Torak slipped and went down on one knee. Struggled to his feet. Glanced over the edge. The bear had climbed a third of the way.

He ran on. He reached the overhang and threw himself into the rocky hollow, bent double, fighting for breath. Now for the rest of his plan: now to call on the Spirit for help.

Forcing himself upright, he filled his chest with air, put back his head and *howled*.

Wolf took up the howl, and their piercing cries buffeted the ravine—back and forth, back and forth through the Mountains. *World Spirit*, howled Torak, *I bring you the Nanuak! Hear me! Send your power to crush the demon from the Forest!*

Below him, he heard the bear getting closer . . . ice clattering into the ravine.

On and on he howled until his ribs ached. *World Spirit, hear my plea. . . .*

Nothing happened.

Torak stopped howling. Horror washed over him. The World Spirit had not answered his plea. The bear was coming for him. . . .

Suddenly he realized that Wolf, too, had stopped howling.

Look behind you, Torak.

He turned to see Hord's axe swinging toward him.

THIRTY-TWO

Torak dodged, and the axe hissed past his ear, splintering the ice where he'd been standing.

Hord wrenched it free. "Give me the Nanuak!" he cried. "*I* have to take it to the Mountain!"

"Get away from me!" said Torak.

From the edge of the ravine came a grinding of ice. The bear was nearing the top.

Hord's haggard face twisted in pain. Torak could barely imagine how he'd brought himself to track them through the demon-haunted Forest; to brave the wrath of the Spirit by venturing up the trail. "*Give me the Nanuak*," repeated Hord.

Wolf advanced on him, his whole body a shuddering snarl. He was no longer a cub; he was a ferocious young wolf defending his pack brother.

Hord ignored him. "I *will* have it! It's my fault this is happening! *I* have to make it end!"

Suddenly, Torak understood. "It was you," he said. "You were there when the bear was made. You were with the Red Deer Clan. You helped the crippled Soul-Eater trap the demon."

"I didn't *know*!" protested Hord. "He said he needed a bear—I caught a young one. I never knew what he meant to do!"

Then several things happened at once. Hord swung his axe at Torak's throat. Torak ducked. Wolf sprang at Hord, sinking his teeth into his wrist. Hord bellowed and dropped his axe, but with his free fist he rained blows on Wolf's unprotected head.

"No!" yelled Torak, drawing his knife and launching himself at Hord. Hord seized Wolf by the scruff and threw him against the basalt, then twisted around and lunged for the Nanuak swinging from Torak's neck.

Torak jerked out of reach. Hord went for his legs, throwing him backward onto the ice. But as Torak went down, he tore the pouch from his neck and hurled it up the trail, out of Hord's reach. Wolf righted himself with a shake and leaped for the pouch, catching it in midair, but landing perilously close to the edge of the ravine.

"Wolf!" cried Torak, struggling beneath Hord, who was straddling his chest and kneeling on his arms.

Wolf's hind paws scrabbled wildly at the edge. From just below him came a menacing growl—then the bear's black claws sliced the air, narrowly missing Wolf's paws. . . .

Wolf gave a tremendous heave and regained the trail. But then, for the first time ever, he decided to *return* something Torak had thrown, and bounded toward him with the Nanuak in his jaws.

Hord strained to reach the pouch. Torak wrested one hand free and dragged his arm away. If only his knife arm wasn't pinned under Hord's knee . . .

An unearthly roar shook the ravine. In horror, Torak watched the bear rise above the edge of the trail.

And in that final moment, as the bear towered above them, as Wolf paused with the Nanuak in his jaws—in that final moment as Torak struggled with Hord, the true meaning of the Prophecy broke upon him. *The Listener gives his heart's blood to the Mountain.*

His heart's blood.

Wolf.

No! he cried inside his head.

But he knew what he had to do. Out loud he shouted to Wolf, "Take it to the Mountain! Uff! Uff! Uff!"

Wolf's golden gaze met his.

"Uff!" gasped Torak. His eyes stung.

Wolf turned and raced up the trail toward the Mountain.

Hord snarled with fury and staggered after him— but he slipped and toppled backward, screaming, into the arms of the bear.

Torak scrambled to his feet. Hord was still screaming. Torak had to help him. . . .

From high above came a deafening crack.

The trail shook. Torak was thrown to his knees.

The crack swelled to a grinding roar. He threw himself beneath the overhang—and an instant later, down came the rushing, rampaging, killing snow, obliterating Hord, obliterating the bear—sending them howling down into death.

The World Spirit had heard Torak's plea.

The last thing Torak saw was Wolf, the Nanuak still in his jaws, racing under the thundering snow toward the Mountain. *Wolf!* he shouted. Then the whole world turned white.

Torak never knew how long he crouched against the rock face, with his eyes tight shut.

At last he became aware that the thundering had turned to echoes—and that the echoes were getting fainter. The World Spirit was striding away into the Mountains.

The sound of its footsteps faded to a hiss of settling snow. . . .

Then a whisper . . .

Then—silence.

Torak opened his eyes.

He could see out across the ravine. He was not buried alive. The World Spirit had passed over the overhang and let him live. But where was Wolf?

He got to his feet and stumbled to the edge of the trail. The dead cold had gone. He saw the Mountains through a haze of settling snow. Below him, the ravine had disappeared under a chaos of ice and rock. Buried beneath it lay Hord and the bear.

Hord had paid with his life. The bear was an empty husk, for the Spirit had banished the demon to the Otherworld. Perhaps the bear's own souls would now be at peace, after their long imprisonment with the demon.

Torak had fulfilled his oath to Fa. He had given the Nanuak to the World Spirit—and the Spirit had destroyed the bear.

He knew that, but he couldn't feel it. All he could feel was the ache in his chest. Where was Wolf? Had he reached the Mountain before the snow came down? Or did he too lie buried under the ice?

"*Please* be alive," murmured Torak. "Please. I'll never ask anything again."

A breeze lifted his hair but brought no answer.

A young crow flew over the Mountains, cawing and sky-dancing with the joy of flight. From the east came a thunder of hooves. Torak knew what that meant. It meant that the reindeer were coming down from the fells. The Forest was returning to life.

Turning, he saw that the way to the south remained open; he would be able to find his way back to Renn and Fin-Kedinn and the Ravens.

Then from the north—beyond the torrent of ice that blocked the trail, behind the clouds that hid the Mountain of the World Spirit—a wolf howled.

It was not the high, wobbly yowl of a cub, but the pure, heart-wrenching song of a young wolf. And yet it was still unmistakably Wolf.

The pain in Torak's chest broke loose and lifted free.

As he listened to the music of Wolf's song, more wolf-voices joined it: weaving in and out, but never drowning that one clear, well-loved voice. Wolf was not alone.

Torak's eyes blurred with tears. He understood. Wolf was howling a farewell. He wasn't coming back.

The howling ceased. Torak bowed his head. "But he's alive," he said out loud. "That's what matters. He is alive."

He longed to howl a reply: to tell Wolf that it was

not forever; that one day, he would find some way for them to be together. But he couldn't think how to say it, because in wolf talk there is no future.

Instead, he said it in his own speech. He knew that Wolf wouldn't understand, but he also knew that he was making the promise to himself as much as to Wolf.

"Someday," he called, and his voice rang through the radiant air, "someday we will be together. We will hunt together in the Forest. Together—" His voice broke. "I *promise*. My brother, the wolf."

No answer came back. But Torak had not expected one. He had made his promise.

He stooped for a handful of snow to cool his burning face. It felt good. He scooped up some more and rubbed the Death Mark from his forehead.

Then he turned and started back toward the Forest.

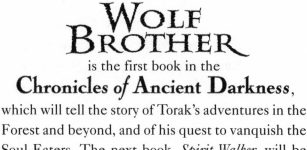

WOLF
BROTHER

is the first book in the
Chronicles *of* Ancient Darkness,
which will tell the story of Torak's adventures in the
Forest and beyond, and of his quest to vanquish the
Soul-Eaters. The next book, *Spirit Walker*, will be
published in 2005.

AUTHOR'S NOTE

If you could go back to Torak's world, you'd find some of it amazingly familiar and some of it utterly strange. You'd have gone back six thousand years, to a time when the Forest covered the whole of northwest Europe. The Ice Age had ended a few thousand years before, so the mammoths and saber-toothed tigers had gone; and although most of the trees, plants, and animals would be the same as they are now, the forest horses would be sturdier, and you'd probably be astonished at your first sight of an auroch: an enormous wild ox, with forward-pointing horns, which stood about six feet high at the shoulder.

The people of Torak's world would look just like you or me, but their way of life would strike you as very different. Hunter-gatherers lived in small clans and moved around a lot: sometimes staying in a campsite only for a few days, like Torak and Fa of the Wolf Clan, or sometimes staying for a whole moon or a season, like the Raven and Boar Clans. They hadn't yet heard of farming, and they didn't have writing, metals, or the wheel. They didn't need them. They were superb survivors. They knew all about the animals, trees, plants, and rocks of the Forest. When they wanted something, they knew where to find it, or how to make it.

Much of this I've been able to learn from archaeology: in other words, from the traces of the clans' weapons, food, clothes, and shelters that they left behind in the Forest. But that's only part of it. How did they *think*? What did they believe about life and death, and where they came from? For that, I've looked at the lives of more recent hunter-gatherers, including some of the Native American tribes, the Inuit (Eskimo), the San of southern Africa, and the Ainu of Japan.

And yet this leaves the question of what it actually *feels* like to live in the Forest. What does spruce resin taste like? Or reindeer heart, or smoked elk? How does it feel to sleep in one of the Raven Clan's open-fronted shelters?

Fortunately, it's possible to find out, at least to some extent, because parts of the Forest still remain. I've been there. And at times, it can take about three seconds to go back six thousand years. If you hear red deer bellowing at midnight, or find fresh wolf tracks crossing your own; if you suddenly have to persuade a very edgy bear that you're neither threat nor prey . . . that's when you're back in Torak's world.

Finally, I'd like to thank some people. I want to thank Jorma Patosalmi for guiding me through the forest of northern Finland, for letting me try out a birch-bark horn, for showing me how to carry fire in a piece of smoldering fungus, and for lots of other hunting hints and Forest tips. I also want to thank Mr. Derrick Coyle, the Yeoman Ravenmaster of the Tower of London, for introducing me to some extremely august ravens. Concerning wolves, I'm deeply indebted to the work of David Mech, Michael Fox, Lois Crisler, and Shaun Ellis. And lastly, I want to thank my agent, Peter Cox, and my editor, Fiona Kennedy, for their unfailing enthusiasm and support.

MICHELLE PAVER, 2004